AND THE MINDMASTER

Morgan Swift has learnt to trust her psychic powers. And so when she sees a strange aura over three of her pupils, her suspicions are aroused. When she finds that their work, usually of a rather average quality, is suddenly outstandingly good, she decides to investigate. The three pupils, she learns, have been taking evening classes with a cult leader called Yang.

Who is Yang, and what is this extraordinary power he has over her pupils? But as Morgan probes further, she arouses Yang's suspicions – and makes herself a very dangerous enemy!

Other titles in this series:

Morgan Swift and the Trail of the Jaguar

Morgan SWIFT

AND THE MINDMASTER

Martine Lesley

**Hippo Books
Scholastic Publications Limited
London**

Scholastic Publications Ltd.,
10 Earlham Street, London WC2H 9RX, UK

Scholastic Inc.,
730 Broadway, New York, NY 10003, USA

Scholastic Tab Publications Ltd.,
123 Newkirk Road, Richmond Hill,
Ontario L4C 3G5, Canada

Ashton Scholastic Pty. Ltd.,
P O Box 579, Gosford, New South Wales,
Australia

Ashton Scholastic Ltd.,
165 Marua Road, Panmure, Auckland 6,
New Zealand

First published by Random House Inc., 1985
Published in paperback by Scholastic Publications Ltd., 1988

Text copyright © Ann M. Martin, 1986

ISBN 0 590 70916 X

Chapter 1

A *flash*.

That was what Morgan Swift called it when she looked at someone and saw that someone's secret self lit up as bright as if a flashbulb had gone off.

Morgan had discovered her weird power at ten, when she opened the front door to a man who said he was a salesman. In a flash she *saw* the evil simmering within him, and slammed the door in his face. A week later she saw his picture in the paper. He had been arrested for a series of violent robberies. And Morgan had her first proof that she could trust her mysterious gift.

By the time Morgan was twenty-four she had seen enough flashes illuminating the most unexpected people at the most unexpected times to make her trust her vision completely.

But she didn't talk about it. For one thing it was the kind of eerie ability that anyone might want to keep private, and Morgan was very private person. For another it would make her job that much harder. A science teacher was supposed to explain strange phenomena, not be one.

As it was, even with her psychic skill kept under wraps, *strange* was a mild word compared with the words used to describe Morgan at Coolidge High School, where she taught science.

1

Undignified. Disruptive. Shocking. Those were words fellow teachers used.

Wild. Fabulous. Super. Those words came from her students.

Teachers and students agreed on one thing, though. Before Morgan's arrival, Coolidge High had never seen a teacher like her.

Her strikingly beautiful face and long-legged athletic figure set her apart at first sight.

Topping that was the startling streak of silver running through her short, almost punk-cut black hair.

Then there were the three earrings she wore, one of them always an exquisitely fashioned golden bee.

And her favorite footwear: red cowboy boots decorated with black roses, custom-made by the legendary San Antonio firm of Lucchese which made boots for presidents, oil sheiks, movie stars, and other very special people all over the world.

Her most treasured piece of clothing: a vintage faded denim jacket still brightened by the psychedelic embroidery of the 1960s, which Morgan thought of as *her* time, even though she had been only ten when the decade ended.

Her car: a gleaming black Mercedes 190 SL two-seater from the same era, kept in mint condition by Morgan's tender, loving overhauls.

Her shoulder bag: made of scuffed tooled leather, and big enough to carry her complete chemistry kit along with a well-worn tarot deck and a dog-eared book on astrology.

Not to mention her casual conversational

references to rock stars and Zen monks she had known, and exotic places from Afghanistan to Zambia she had visited.

Put them all together and they added up to someone who was definitely not what the middle-of-the-road school system of the middle-sized Massachusetts city of Langford expected a teacher to be – except in one respect. Students in her classes wound up learning more than they and their other teachers ever suspected they could. Which was why, even after two years of shaking up the school scene, Morgan kept a firm hold on her job.

Right now, though, it was Morgan who was shaken up – and had to keep a firm hold on herself to keep from showing it.

She had been hit not by one flash but by three, one right after another, out of the blue.

She was looking at three students in her tenth-grade chemistry class. Or rather, she was looking at the tops of their heads as they bent over the test they were taking.

The three sat side by side in the first row.

Amy Parsons, her face framed by long, wavy brown hair, and her dramatic good looks matching her talent as star actress of the school drama club.

Carl Meyer, tall, red-haired, freckle-faced, and already as a second-year a key player on the football, basketball, and baseball teams.

Sam Higgenbottom, short, wiry, his hair in a modified Afro, his skin almost as dark as the black frames of the oversized glasses that gave him a scholarly appearance to go with his reputation as the class brain.

Morgan's eyes moved from one to another of those three, trying to make sense of what she saw.

She saw over each of their heads an eerie light – almost like the glow from a television screen. She peered into that light and saw a vaguely defined shape – the same shape above all three of the kids. Morgan strained to make it out more clearly. It was a face, definitely a face, but the features remained obscured. Morgan tried harder. She could see a mouth moving, two eyes dark as night, and then – nothing.

The flash was over.

Morgan was disappointed, but not surprised. Her flashes never lasted long, just long enough to wake her to danger. After that, it was up to her to figure out what the danger was, and what to do about it.

Morgan was charged up now, from the tips of her red boots to the top of the silver streak in her hair. The green flecks in her eyes brightened and stood out like emerald chips, the way they did when she was thinking hard and fast.

Morgan had no idea whose face she'd seen in the flash. But she didn't like the idea of it hovering over the three kids.

The way she saw it, someone or something might be trying to control them – and in Morgan's eyes, anyone or anything that tried to take control of kids was bad news.

But who or what was it? And why these three?

Morgan started to put together what she knew about them. It was like filling in the blanks of a crossword puzzle that contained a

4

secret message.

Already Morgan could figure out that the three must be hanging out together. They were sitting side by side in her class by choice, since she let kids sit where they wanted, rather than sticking them in slots dictated by their grades, or the alphabet, or her whims.

Funny, she thought. She had never figured them to be that close. They each belonged to a different clique. Amy was in the theatre crowd. Carl hung out with the lads. And Sam was part of a group noted for high marks, thick glasses, and a total disregard for everything but their favourite school subjects – in short, the group that other kids called the nerds.

Something had brought these three together and was holding them together.

But what?

Morgan stared hard – but there were no more flashes, not even when she could look into her students' faces, rather than seeing just the tops of their heads, after the bell rang and they came to her desk with the others in the class to drop off their test papers.

The three of them rose to their feet at the same instant and delivered their papers one right after the other.

First Amy.

"How did it go?" Morgan asked.

"Oh, okay, I guess," Amy said with a relaxed smile that not even as good an actress as she could have faked.

Next came Carl.

"I hope you finally mastered the periodic tables," said Morgan.

"No sweat," said Carl, looking as cool as he did when he took a free throw on the basketball court.

"I won't ask how you did, Sam," Morgan said. "No problem, I presume."

"No problem," Sam agreed, looking as if he didn't have a care in the world as he followed the others out of the room.

It was Morgan who had the problem.

Had she been imagining things in her flash?

Or were her eyes deceiving her as she looked into the kids' untroubled faces?

She would have to go over their test papers carefully. Maybe in their answers she would find answers of her own.

But that night, when she did so, she only found other, even more puzzling questions.

Chapter 2

Morgan Swift's flat was basically one very large room. Together with a tiny kitchen and a modest bathroom, it took up the entire top floor of a Victorian mansion that had been broken up into flats after the last surviving member of an old New England family sold it to a real estate developer.

The flat now looked like nothing that either the former residents or the new owner would ever have dreamed of.

The walls and ceiling were a many-coated white so pure that they seemed to be melting into empty space. There were no carpets on the floor to mask the glowing natural colour of the richly polished wood. Overhead a translucent Japanese paper globe softened the electric light that gently washed the room. On the walls were three pictures. One, from India, was of a smiling goddess with a flower in one hand and a sword in another standing beside a tree whose thickly foliaged limbs were weighed down with countless exotic birds. The second, a poster advertising a Police concert, showed only the name of the band in huge red letters on a background of electric blue, and a personal dedication to Morgan written in white crayon by Sting himself. The third was a small oil painting of a strikingly handsome Renaissance prince that, though incongruous in this modern

7

setting, undeniably looked like an original.

The furniture was minimal. A rolled-up Japanese mat that was unrolled each night to serve as a bed. A round, claw-legged antique oak table surrounded by four captain's chairs. A low, pearl-grey couch. And a square white parson's table big enough to hold a state-of-the-art personal computer and printer and still give Morgan all the work space she needed.

Morgan was at her work table now. In front of her were the test papers that Amy, Carl, and Sam had handed in that day.

She was trying to make sense of their scores – and couldn't.

Sam's results weren't any problem. Science was his strong suit, and he seldom gave a wrong answer. Morgan couldn't see anything wrong with his perfect score this time.

But both Amy and Carl were very different from Sam, and normally their test scores were just as different.

The only chemistry that Amy really cared about was the chemistry between herself and her audience when she was onstage. But on this test she had scored a ninety, her highest mark of the school year.

Normally Carl wasn't much better. He preferred working out on the ball field to exercising his brain in the lab. But on this test he had got all but three questions right. That gave him a ninety-four.

Morgan's brows knitted. Had Amy and Carl cheated?

It was an ugly possibility – but it was the first one that Morgan had to consider.

She examined it as carefully as if she were looking at it through her microscope. And she felt both relieved and perplexed when the closer she looked, the smaller the chances of cheating appeared.

On her tests, Morgan always included a couple of questions to reward students who did work on their own – questions that students who merely followed the material covered in class could never answer.

On this test, Sam had got both those questions right. Neither Amy nor Carl had.

Of course, the pair of them might have been clever enough not to want to get a suspiciously perfect score. They might have ignored the answers to questions they could not possibly have known. But how good at cheating could a couple of beginners be? Morgan knew from their previous dismal test scores that they could never have cheated in her class before.

Even more convincing evidence of their innocence came from the other questions they had missed.

Amy had missed three other questions. Carl had missed one other – and it was different from any of the ones that Amy had got wrong.

As far as Morgan could see, that ruled out cheating. She had to look elsewhere for an explanation.

She looked more closely at the questions Amy had missed. All had to do with the sizes and masses of oleic acid molecules.

On a sudden hunch, Morgan switched on her desk-top computer and requested the dates she had covered oleic acid in class.

The display screen flashed: FEB 4, FEB 5.

Then Morgan requested Amy's attendance record in class.

The answer that she already half expected came instantly: DAYS ABSENT: FEB 4, FEB 5.

Morgan remembered that Amy had stayed home with the 'flu those two days.

Morgan followed the same process in checking out Carl's error, that one having to do with lead nitrate.

Morgan had covered lead nitrate on March 4. Carl had missed class that day because of a state basketball tournament final in another city.

Morgan had her explanation for all the errors that the two kids had made. But she still had no explanation at all for all the questions they had got right. She still had to figure out how for the first time in their school lives Amy and Carl had absorbed everything taught in class. Morgan liked to think of herself as a good teacher, but she knew she wasn't *that* good.

She stared a moment at the computer screen as if hoping it would tell her more of its own accord. Of course, it couldn't. You only got out of it what you put into it. She had filled it with a lot of facts just for fun, but she needed different facts now, facts she could work with.

"Hey, can you tell me what's wrong with these kids who got everything right? Or do you think I'm crazy, worrying because they did *too* too well?" Morgan asked her two cats, Twist and Shout. They stood side by side, regarding her unusual late-night activity with curiosity and some suspicion.

Twist, a sleek brown Abyssinian, responded to Morgan's questions by licking her paw industriously. Shout, a large, tough-looking, black-and-white alley cat, gave an elaborate yawn.

"You're right. It's time for bed," conceded Morgan with a grin.

She switched off the computer with a flick of her finger. Then she lay down and did a series of yoga exercises that slowed and then turned off her racing mind and let her plunge into a deep and dreamless sleep. There was nothing more she could find out about Amy and Carl and Sam until the next day.

Early the next day, by the light of dawn.

When once again Morgan was off and running, pursuing answers as elusive as a phantom face seen in a flash.

Chapter 3

Morgan had to keep her speed down when she ran with Jeff Collins.

Jeff was the Coolidge High P.E. instructor and athletic coach. He had been a pretty fair athlete in college and had kept himself in good shape since. But on their regular Tuesday and Friday early morning ten-mile runs together, he was no match for Morgan.

By now he had learned better than to challenge her by quickening the pace. He had been left gasping in her trail too many times when she responded by pulling out all the stops of her remarkable speed and endurance.

The only challenge he tried to offer her now was when he urged her to go into big-time running. He mentioned Mary Decker and Joan Benoit. He talked about fame and fortune. He offered to be her coach and manager. He even hinted strongly that he would be glad to play an even more important role than that in her life.

Morgan simply answered that she preferred to keep things the way they were, running for the pure joy of it and enjoying his company as a friend and fellow runner.

At the same time she was careful to keep her running under control. Watching Jeff get red in the face while his eyes blinked away the sweat and his strained smile tried to say that everything was just fine was not one of Morgan's favourite sights.

This dawn-lit morning she ran by Jeff's side a beat slower than usual so that he would have enough breath to answer her questions.

One question, really, after she set it up by asking about the baseball team's prospects for the coming season.

"How is Carl Meyer shaping up?" she asked. "He's the big hope of your pitching staff, isn't he?"

"Sure is," said Jeff. "The kid's shaping up just great. I gotta say, I was worried about him for nothing."

"What was the problem?" Morgan asked, almost nonchalantly.

"His control," Jeff said. "I mean, Carl's a great natural athlete, and as a pitcher, he's got all the speed he needs. He's even learning how to break off a pretty good curve ball, though I don't let him do it too much, because his arm is a little too young for it. But he has had this control problem."

"Wild, huh?" said Morgan, slowing the pace even more.

"He'd walk as many batters as he'd strike out," said Jeff. "I think it all started when he hit a batter with a fastball in a first-year game early last season. The other kid got off with just a bruise, but after that, Carl seemed afraid to get the ball over the inside corner of the plate. Up until this year, at least."

"He's okay now?"

"Like he was cured overnight," said Jeff. "One day he was as wild as ever. The next day he had pinpoint control, as if he didn't have a

13

fear in the world."

"When did that happen?"

"Just last week. It was like a miracle – though of course it really wasn't. I've been coaching kids long enough to know that. Kids can get rid of hangups by simply growing out of them – real sudden like."

Then he grinned at Morgan. "Hey, baby, you must be getting out of shape. You're going at a real turtle's pace."

Morgan grinned back.

"We'll see who's the turtle," she said.

By the time they finished their run a half hour later, Jeff was gasping like a turtle that had been turned over on its shell in the sun.

"Me and my big mouth," he said.

Morgan didn't tell him that she appreciated his big mouth. He had filled in another blank in the puzzle of Carl and the others.

The trouble was, the more blanks that were filled in, the less she could see.

Carl was not only doing better in her class, he was also doing better on the ball field. How could she find anything wrong with that?

She certainly couldn't expect Jeff to. She was sure he had never had a flash in his life – expect maybe about whether a pitcher would come in with a fastball or a curve.

She'd have to continue on her hunt alone.

It was Friday, her day to meet Peter Enders for lunch in the teachers' dining room. Peter – no one would ever think of calling him Pete – had made this lunch a standing date, in addition to the dates he had with Morgan when a concert or an art show or any other cultural event took place in Langford. As far as Peter was concerned, Morgan was practically the only other teacher at Coolidge to truly appreciate "the finer things in life," including the poetry he himself wrote when not teaching English.

Actually, as a poet, he wasn't too bad. Not only did he look the part, being tall and thin and having a beard that added strength to his sensitive face, he even produced decent poems. Unfortunately, Morgan had to keep from complimenting them too highly. Lately his poems had begun to deal with his warm feelings for an unnamed young lady with a silver streak in her black hair and flecks of green in her hazel eyes. Morgan preferred that that young lady remained nameless and that Peter's feelings didn't boil over.

Today Morgan didn't give him a chance to read his latest poems to her.

As soon as she saw him reaching for his briefcase to pull out the typewritten sheets of paper stored there, she said, "Look, Peter, I need some information. I wonder if you could help me."

"As they put it in the eighteenth century, I am your humble and obedient servant," Peter said. Peter could be trusted never to say anything in one word when he could say it in ten.

"Three of my students – Amy Parsons, Carl Meyer, and Sam Higgenbottom – have started to do extremely well in my class," Morgan said. "I want to find out whether it's because of some new teaching methods I've been experimenting with, or whether they've simply become better students on their own. How are they doing in your class?"

"Morgan, I'm sure your mere presence in class would be all the inspiration any student would need," Peter said. "Why, just sitting here across the table from you, I feel –"

"Thanks, Peter," Morgan said. "I appreciate the compliments. But answers are what I need."

"There are times, Morgan, when your practicality is overwhelming," said Peter, shrugging. "Okay, if dull facts are what you want, dull facts are what I'll give you. Actually, though, they aren't that dull. The three students you mentioned have started doing interesting work – especially Sam. I mean, Amy's always been a star English student, so good work from her isn't very surprising. And though Carl's work has improved, it really isn't very spectacular. But Sam is the big surprise. I know he's some kind of genius in science, but he's always had trouble expressing himself in anything other than the driest, most matter-of-fact way in his English essays. Lately, though, his work has changed radically."

"How so?" Morgan leaned forward, already sensing what she was about to hear.

"His writing in his class assignments has become extraordinarily expressive, full of sensitive emotion as well as cold facts, and he makes wonderful links between his personal experiences and whatever subject he's writing about. I have to confess that, when this change first came over his work, I suspected he might be cheating, either stealing from a book or else having another student write his compositions for him. But when his work stayed on the same high level in a classroom essay test, I was convinced he was doing it on his own."

"When did this change start to happen?" asked Morgan.

"Quite recently, a couple of weeks ago," said Peter. "It was as if a tap inside him had suddenly been turned on, and his talent came pouring out. That's the great thing about watching students mature. They're full of such great surprises. You can never tell ahead of time what's really inside them."

"You never can tell," Morgan agreed, and changed the subject. Peter had told her all he could.

There was one more teacher Morgan wanted to question, and Morgan spotted her taking a coffee break in the teachers' lounge that afternoon.

She was Mrs Avery, the school drama teacher. Morgan didn't even have to ask her about Amy Parsons. All Morgan had to do was break the ice by asking about the big school spring show that was coming up, and Mrs Avery did the rest.

"The play is going simply *swim*mingly," said Mrs Avery. It had been at least ten years since Mrs Avery had abandoned her summer stock and winter starvation acting carèer to take up teaching, but she remained permanently on stage, even in a casual conversation like this. "I was prepared for such a *struggle* to cast the production. You know, this year we're doing a musical, *The Wiz*, and the lead actress has a simply *crush*ing role, with one big number after

17

another. I didn't know *whom* I could find to fit the part, when suddenly Amy Parsons came up with a simply *stun*ning audition. I was *flab*bergasted. Amy has always been a talented actress, of course, but her singing voice always used to be, well *small*. Perhaps *timid* would be a better word. Now, suddenly, she sounded like Diana Ross belting out a song. Wait until you see the show. It'll be an absolute *smash*. And wait until you hear Amy. You'll be amazed!"

"I can hardly wait," said Morgan, who could hardly wait to end this conversation and go on with the next stage of her investigation.

She had found out all she could from her fellow teachers. All they could see was that something very good was happening to Carl and Amy and Sam.

If she wanted to find out more, she had to get a different point of view.

And she knew where to get it.

Chapter 4

If you met Sally Jackson and Jenny Wu separately, you'd never figure them to be best friends.

Sally was voted the prettiest girl in the tenth grade and dressed the part, having already begun a career as a teen model. Jenny, whose parents came from Taiwan, was pretty too, but did not use a trace of makeup, tied her hair in a practical ponytail, and wore the same slightly oversized jeans day after day. Sally was the school's head cheerleader. Jenny was champion of the chess club. Sally was dated up months in advance by a long string of admirers; Jenny preferred doing advanced maths problems on Saturday night.

But best friends they definitely were – through a kind of chemistry that even Morgan Swift would have found hard to analyze.

They simply *liked* each other and wanted the best for each other. Sally urged Jenny to make better use of her looks, and Jenny urged Sally to make better use of her mind. They lent each other their favourite records and listened to them together, lent each other their favourite books and magazines and talked about them together, and watched each other's favourite TV shows together. Even when they disagreed about something, each had a strong hunch the other's opinion might more than likely be absolutely right, but one thing they didn't disagree about at all was Morgan Swift. They both thought that she was the best thing ever to happen to Coolidge High.

The year before, they had been in Morgan's general science class. This year they were enjoying Morgan's chemistry class even more. They actually looked forward to staying after school to work on lab assignments – partly for the fun of solving the chemistry problems that Morgan had set up and partly because Morgan was there to help them do them.

Today, though, it was Morgan who was asking for their help.

They were cleaning up their work area when Morgan came over to them and asked, "Look, could you give me some info about the school social scene? I thought I had a good line on the different cliques – but now I'm not so sure."

Seeing their puzzled expressions, Morgan explained, "I'm talking about Amy Parsons and Carl Meyer and Sam Higgenbottom. I never thought they were close friends, but lately I've noticed them hanging out together. At the same time their grades have taken a big jump. I was wondering if they've formed some kind of study group. I mean, something like that would be a great idea – but it would really surprise me. I'd have to revise all my ideas about students at Coolidge."

"Me too," Sally said with a grin.

"I can't see them doing that," agreed Jenny. "On the other hand, they *have* been hanging out together a lot lately. I didn't think much about it, but now that you mention it, it does seem strange."

"A mystery," said Sally.

"A mystery I'd really like to solve," said Morgan. She paused. "Look, I know that kids aren't supposed to spy on other kids for teachers – even if the teacher isn't looking for anything wrong happening, but just wants to know what *is* happening . . ."

Morgan let her voice trail off, and looked at Sally and Jenny.

The two girls started to speak at once. They stopped, and Sally told Jenny to go first.

"I'd be glad to help, " said Jenny. "Like you said, it wouldn't be tattling – just gathering information. Besides, you've made me kind of curious myself – like when you give us a problem in class. It makes me want to find the solution."

"And it's not like you're an ordinary teacher," said Sally. "I mean, it's like you're more on the kids' side than on the teachers' side. Not that you're like a kid, either, of course. I guess what I'm trying to say is, you're just *you*."

"Thanks for the compliment – if it is one," said Morgan. "And thanks for the offer of help. I can use it. You can find out what those guys are into a lot easier than I can."

Morgan was right. In fact, it turned out to be easier than Sally and Jenny imagined.

They had barely left the lab when they saw Amy, Carl, and Sam standing in front of a locker. Sally and Jenny looked at each other, nodded, and without saying a word headed for the three kids.

"Hi," Sally said to them. "What's happening?"

"What're you up to? Anything interesting?" Jenny asked. "I mean, this school year is really dragging. It's getting to be such a *bore*."

The three kids didn't hesitate in answering.

"Not for us," Amy said.

"Never had such a good year," said Carl.

"The best," said Sam.

"Let us in on your secret," said Sally.

"Yeah, it sounds like you've struck gold somewhere," said Jenny.

"Unless, of course, you don't want to share it," Sally said with a mock shrug.

"We'd be glad to share it," said Amy.

"In fact, we're *supposed* to share it," said Carl.

"Yang calls it 'spreading the light'," said Sam.

"Yang? Who's Yang?" asked Jenny.

"He's our teacher," said Amy.

"Except he doesn't like to be called our teacher," said Carl.

"Right," said Sam. "He doesn't like titles. He says they've been abused by too many people, whether they call themselves teachers, or gurus, or masters. He says he's just an instrument to tap the power we already have – a key we can use to let that power out."

"Sounds kind of weird to me," said Sally.

"Bizarre," agreed Jenny.

"That's what I thought when Carl told me about him," said Amy.

"And what I said when Amy told me," said Sam.

"I didn't believe it myself when I first went to

22

him," Carl said. "In fact, I wouldn't have gone to him at all if I hadn't been so desperate. But after my pitching went out of whack, I was willing to try anything to get my control back. So when a member of the basketball team told me how Yang had helped improve his foul shots, I thought, why not give it a try? So I did, and it's not only my baseball that's got better – it's everything."

"That's what happens." agreed Amy. "I went to Yang to help my singing – but so much more has been improved."

"I was worried about my marks in English – I thought they'd keep me from getting into M.I.T.," said Sam. "Now it'll be a snap."

"Hey, this Yang guy seems too good to be true," said Sally.

"Sure you're not being paid to do his P.R.?" said Jenny.

"That's the trouble," said Sam. "It does sound too good to be true. You have to see it to believe it."

"But you can do that easily enough," said Amy. "We're going to Yang's right now. Come along and see."

"Of course, you won't be able to see as much as we do – at first," said Carl.

"But someday maybe you'll be able to – if you qualify," said Sam.

"I *knew* there had to be a hitch," said Jenny.

"Yeah," said Sally, grimacing. "We have to pass some kind of entrance exam, right?"

"Not at all," Sam said. "Everyone is welcome at Yang's classes. It's just that there are different levels of instruction."

"That's right," said Amy. "You can't walk before you crawl."

"Or run before you walk," said Carl.

"But you can take the first step now," said Amy.

"Come on," said Carl.

"Why wait?" said Sam.

"Okay," said Jenny.

"We will," said Sally.

They traded quick glances as they followed Amy, Carl, and Sam out of the school building.

They could hardly wait to find out who this Yang guy was and what he did.

Even more, they could hardly wait to tell Morgan.

Chapter 5

Morgan Swift was standing on her head when her phone rang.

It was her favourite yoga position. It relaxed her body and cleared her mind. Even more important, it let her look at things from a different point of view.

That was the way, she knew, to approach a difficult problem, like the problem she faced now as she tried to figure out if anything was really threatening the three kids in her class. You had to look at a problem like that from different angles until you could spot the answer.

As soon as she heard the phone, she did a neat flip and landed on her feet. She picked up the phone before it could ring again.

"Hello."

"Hi," said Sally's voice. "I hope I didn't disturb you, calling you at night and all."

"No sweat," said Morgan. "Coolidge High lets me stay up late on Friday nights – it's written into my contract. Tell me, what did you find out?"

"We found out *everything*," said Sally.

Sally paused, and Morgan said, "Don't keep me in suspense. Tell me about it."

"The thing is, it would be kind of hard to do over the phone," Sally said. "There's so much to tell, and I'm sure Jenny has things she'd like to add to whatever I could say. We could wait until we see you in school on Monday – or if you'd like, we could come over now to where you live. Jenny's spending the night at my house, and my parents will be out until real late, so nobody has to know about our undercover spying mission and our top-secret report."

"Tonight would be fine," Morgan said, and gave Sally her address.

"We'll be there in half an hour," Sally said.

It took them just twenty minutes, riding their bikes in tenth gear all the way.

Morgan saw them both glancing around as they entered her apartment. Their glances were quick, almost furtive. They didn't want to be too open about their curiosity. It didn't bother Morgan, though. She was used to curiosity, and she didn't really mind it. She figured it was part of the price she had to pay for choosing to live in a slightly different way from most people in order to be her own person. People were bound to be curious, whether they were envious, angered, or simply admiring.

Right now Morgan had her own curiosity to satisfy.

"What did you find out?" she asked. "Was I right about Amy and Carl and Sam forming some kind of study group? Or are they into something else?"

"You were right about them being in a group," said Sally, trying to unglue her eyes from the autographed Police poster on Morgan's wall. "Except it's not just them in the group."

"There are about forty kids in it," said Jenny. "And you couldn't really call it a study group."

"It's more like a group that's learning *how to*

26

study," said Sally. "That, and a lot of other things."

"Yang says it will help you do everything better – if you follow his instructions," said Jenny.

"Yang?" said Morgan.

"He's the leader – the teacher, I guess you'd call him," said Jenny. "Though he does have assistants."

"And what does he teach the kids to do?" asked Morgan. "I'm assuming that you found out. It sounds like you got inside wherever he teaches."

"It's a big old house in the old part of town," said Sally. "Yang calls it his Higher Consciousness Centre."

"Did you have any trouble getting in?"

"It would have been hard to stay outside once the front door opened," said Sally. "We got a really warm welcome. They insisted we come in. I must admit, I was kind of nervous going into the place. From the outside, it looked spooky, like one of those houses that little kids like to pretend are haunted. But once we were inside, there was absolutely nothing to be nervous about."

"They had it fixed up really nice," said Jenny. "White ceilings and walls. Hardly any furniture. Some Chinese watercolours and scrolls on the walls. A few vases with flowers or stalks of grain." Jenny looked around her. "Actually, it was a lot like this. I mean, you'd probably feel totally at home there."

"Maybe I'll apply for a job," said Morgan. "Do they have any science classes there?"

Morgan kept her tone light to mask her growing uneasiness. The more she heard, the more she had the feeling that something was askew.

"We just got to sit in on a beginner's class – so we really can't tell you what they teach the kids who have reached a higher level," said Sally. "That includes Amy and Carl and Sam. They've reached the highest level there is. They study under Yang himself on one of the upper floors. Yang put Jenny and me in a ground-floor group that was led by one of his assistants."

"But even that was really interesting," said Jenny.

"He showed us some mental exercises to get rid of all the garbage that clutters up our minds," said Sally. "I had no idea how much there was. I found out what it's like to empty my mind of all the words that keep rattling around inside, just making noise, so it's like I can't hear myself think. It feels great to get rid of that noise, even for a few minutes."

"Then he showed us some physical exercises to go with the mental ones," Jenny said "He said that the mind and the body have to be trained together, because you need one to strengthen the other."

Sally grinned. "By the end of two hours he actually had me standing on my head. Amazing! I never thought I'd find myself doing *that*. I mean, it looks so weird. But you know what? It feels great!"

"So I've heard," said Morgan.

"You really should try it – it's a definite upper," said Jenny. "After two whole hours of

28

exercises, I had more energy than when I started. It was like having my batteries recharged. I can see why Amy and Carl and Sam were so high on the centre, and why they practically twisted our arms to come there with them."

"So they recruited you," said Morgan.

"I guess you could say that," said Jenny. "But 'recruited' sounds so, well, *sinister*. And I couldn't see anything sinister at the centre. Believe me, I looked."

"We both did," said Sally. "I mean, we've heard about cults that brainwash kids and all. But it wasn't like that. It was like the kids told us it would be. And according to them, it keeps getting better the higher you go."

"You sound like you're thinking of going back there," said Morgan.

"It might be worth checking out," said Sally. "I asked the instructor if the classes would help me relax and look natural for the camera when I get jobs doing modelling, and he told me that was one of the goals – to eliminate all the barriers that keep one's total beauty from shining through."

"I didn't have to ask him if it would help my maths and my chess," said Jenny. "I could already feel how much better my mind was functioning, like a computer with the power turned way up. I'd like to find out what a few more sessions would do. What do I have to lose?"

"Just your tuition," said Morgan. "By the way, what do these classes cost?"

"That's the beautiful part," said Jenny. "Nothing."

"*Nothing?*" said Morgan.

"Nothing," Jenny repeated.

"That's right – they're absolutely free!" said Sally.

"I couldn't believe it either, at first," Jenny said, seeing Morgan's surprise. "But when I asked Yang about it, he said that the payment of money interfered with the flow of communication between teacher and students. He said that the only reward a teacher should seek was to see his students learn. He said that his centre supported itself through the generosity of former students who had gone on to financially benefit from their instruction."

"He also said that the centre didn't really need much money, anyway," Sally said. "He and his assistants have freed themselves of the greed for possessions that enslaves so many people."

"I mean, you can't argue with that," said Jenny, challenging the doubt she saw in Morgan's eyes.

"It may sound too good to be true," said Sally.

"But you just have to see it to believe it," said Jenny.

"Right," Morgan said. "I guess I'll have to go to Yang's Higher Consciousness Centre and see for myself."

Chapter 6

On the next day, Saturday, three people received phone calls from Morgan Swift.

One was John Parsons, Amy's father, president of the Langford First National Bank.

Another was Melissa Meyer, Carl's mother. Divorced, she had raised Carl alone while building a practice as one of the city's leading doctors.

The third was Jason Higgenbottom, Sam's father, a successful attorney who was being considered as a candidate for mayor in the next election.

Morgan asked them all the same question. Did they have any suspicions or misgivings about the Higher Consciousness Centre that their children were attending?

All of them did. They knew about the dangers of cults for kids. But none of them had enough hard evidence of anything wrong at the centre to forbid their kids from going, especially since their kids had started to do so well in school by using what they learned there.

Still, all the parents appreciated Morgan's concern. And they urged Morgan to tell them at once if she discovered anything wrong going on.

After Morgan made her last call, she had one more thing to do to prepare herself for her visit to the centre.

She took her deck of tarot cards out of her

shoulder bag. She dealt them out face-down in a pentagonal pattern on the tabletop. She let her hand move over the cards until she could feel a downward pull. She let her hand follow that force until it came down to rest on a card. She flipped the card over.

Even before she saw the card face, she sensed what it would be.

It showed a picture of a robed youth with one arm extended upward, his hand holding a wand pointed towards the heavens. The other arm extended in the opposite direction, with a finger pointing towards the earth. Beside the figure was a table on which were scientific instruments, magical devices, a crude wooden club and an ornate sword.

It was the Magician.

It was *her* card. The symbol of someone who had the knowledge and skill to command the forces of the physical world and of the invisible world.

Now it seemed that it was Yang's card as well.

But *this* card was upside down, reversed. According to the tarot, Yang used the same powers that she did – but for different ends.

Evil ends.

But what on earth can that evil be? Morgan wondered. *All I've heard about this guy are things I approve of. His methods. His results. All I can see when I try to imagine him is somebody very much like me. But that's what the tarot says too. He is like me* – reversed. My mirror image.

But an hour later, when Morgan was ushered into the Higher Consciousness Centre by one of Yang's assistants, Morgan discovered that looking Yang in the face wasn't at all like looking in the mirror.

Sally and Jenny had prepared Morgan for the mansion that housed Yang's centre – a big, slighty sagging, white-shingled old place surrounded by a white picket fence – but they hadn't prepared her for Yang.

To look Yang in the face, Morgan had to lift her gaze sharply upward. Morgan stood five-feet-nine, but Yang was close to seven feet.

Yang inclined his face to gaze down on Morgan. His smile was soothing. His yellowish skin was unlined, giving no clue to his age. His head was shaved, gleaming in the sunlight that poured in through a window. But Morgan barely noticed any of that. What drew her gaze like a magnet were Yang's eyes.

They were not dark, as Morgan expected. They were the purest of blues. Looking into them was like looking into a profoundly blue sky. If Morgan had hoped for a flash about Yang, she knew instantly she was bound to be disappointed. It was all she could do to keep her vision in even normal focus faced with the blinding power of that dazzling blue as Yang's eyes locked with hers.

Thrown off balance, Morgan blinked, turned her eyes away – and Yang inclined his head still farther in a bow of welcome.

"To what do we owe the honour of your visit?" he asked. His voice was deep, his English fluent, though it did have an accent. Morgan could hear a hint of the Far East, along with a definite British shading.

"I teach at Coolidge High School," Morgan

33

said. "Some students have been telling me how much they've got out of your programme. I'm very interested in mind expansion myself, and I thought I'd come here to enquire about enrolling."

"I am deeply grateful for any praise that my students have seen fit to bestow," said Yang. "And I am highly flattered by your interest. Unfortunately, for the moment my programme is open only to those who are sixteen years of age and under. We have only limited teaching resources at present, and experience has shown us that young people's minds are much more flexible and open to improvement than those whose patterns of thought have grown rigid with age. As the centre expands we will be happy to accommodate all those who come seeking enlightenment. That, of course, includes you, Miss –?"

"Swift. Morgan B. Swift," said Morgan. "But, gee, that's bad news. I was really looking forward to seeing what you had to offer. Perhaps if you could tell me something about your programme, it would make waiting to get in a little easier." Morgan gave him her most winning smile. It seemed to work.

"Of course, I will be delighted to tell you all I can," said Yang. "Come, let us share a cup of tea."

Yang led Morgan into a small adjoining room. In it was a low teak table surrounded by cushions. Yang sat cross-legged on one, and Morgan sat opposite him. The same assistant who had opened the door brought in a beautiful blue-glazed teapot and eggshell-thin porcelain

34

teacups, then left the room.

Yang poured tea for them both. He took a small sip of the steaming liquid, and Morgan joined him.

"Delicious," Morgan said. "Delicate, yet somehow powerful. I've never tasted anything like it."

"It is quite rare," said Yang. "It comes from Tibet. It is perhaps a foolish luxury, but I developed a taste for it as a child."

"You grew up in Tibet?" asked Morgan.

"Not exactly," said Yang. "I grew up in Sikkim, a small mountain kingdom bordering Tibet. My father was a Chinese scholar who was living in exile, and my mother was an English-woman who was born in India at the time of the British Empire. I tell you these personal details, boring as they may be, in order to help you understand the roots of my teachings. My centre tries to combine the wisdom of China, India, Tibet and the West. My goal is to offer my students all that human beings have learned about unlocking the power that we all possess yet too seldom fully use."

"You mean it's like some kind of religion?" asked Morgan, making her voice sound be-wildered.

"*Please*, do not make that mistake," said Yang, spreading his hands in gentle supplica-tion. "We here at the centre must constantly struggle against that misconception, lest parents fear we are some kind of dangerous cult and refuse to let their children come to us."

"Well, there *are* some pretty weird groups around," said Morgan.

"Unfortunately, that is true," said Yang. "And no one condemns those groups more strongly than I. But I assure you, what we seek to do with our students is entirely wholesome. We provide them with techniques developed by the wisest of teachers over thousands of years so that young people of today can develop both mind and body in perfect harmony."

"That sounds *super*," said Morgan. "It's *exactly* what I've been looking for practically my whole life. Are you *sure* you can't fit me into one of your classes?"

Yang looked at her as if considering her request – and his eyes met Morgan's once again.

Morgan saw her own eyes reflected in his gleaming pupils and realized he was looking into them as if trying to read her very mind. Then she realized that he could see she was doing the same thing to him.

She averted her probing gaze instantly. But it was too late.

"I am so sorry, Miss Swift," Yang said, "but as I said, we do not have the resources to handle someone like you at the moment, much as we would like to. Perhaps someday . . ." He let his voice trail off as he rose to his feet. "Now if you will excuse me, I have much work to do."

Morgan started to get up too, just as Yang came around the table to assist her.

As she rose, her leg struck the edge of the low table, rattling the teacups.

"Ouch!" she said, losing her balance. She grabbed at Yang's arm to keep from falling, and her hand closed on his wrist.

"I'm *so* sorry!" Morgan exclaimed as they

36

both stared down to where her nails were digging into his flesh.

She released her grip.

"How can I apologize for being so clumsy?" Morgan said, clearly embarrassed.

Yang smiled. "Think nothing more about it, Miss Swift. Accidents will happen." His smile grew broader. "Yes, accidents will happen."

Chapter 7

It was no accident that the big black Cadillac was behind Morgan's Mercedes 190 SL as she headed back toward her flat. Morgan had first seen the car parked across the street from Yang's Higher Consciousness Centre. She saw it next when she looked in her rearview mirror. It was following her.

Morgan sped up, and the Caddy sped up too. She slowed, and it slowed. She swung sharply around a corner, and a moment later it made the same turn.

She didn't like the look of the car, or of its driver, a bearded young man wearing mirrored aviator sunglasses. Nor did she like the fact that there was not another soul in sight as she and the car behind her drove through the grimy, deserted streets of the city's factory district.

"Come on, Morgan, get a hold of yourself, you've been watching too much TV," Morgan told herself. "There isn't going to be any big car chase. Nobody is going to try to run you off the road. That guy's just following you to find out where you're going. You pressed Yang a little too hard, you put him on his guard, that's all. He wouldn't be trying any rough stuff. Not so soon. Not right in the middle of the city."

On the other hand, she might be wrong.

She didn't want to find out the hard way – especially when it would be so easy to shake the guy. Not to mention fun. She didn't often get a chance to show what she and her car could do when challenged. The last time had been winning a vintage-auto road race, and that was more than a year ago.

Morgan pressed down hard on the accelerator. The Mercedes shot forward and whipped around a corner on two wheels. Halfway down the block she braked to a sharp halt and in her rearview mirror saw the Caddy come barrelling around the corner.

The driver's mouth came open as he saw her parked in front of him. He slammed on his brakes, but the momentum of the big car was too powerful. The Caddy skidded out of control – right over the curb and into a sidewalk mailbox. The mailbox crumbled as the Caddy hit it and rolled partly over it. The Caddy came to a halt with the wreck of the mailbox under it lifting and tilting its body so that one of its front wheels hung useless in empty air.

Morgan was almost sorry it had ended so quickly. She had a few more stunts in mind.

There was nothing left to do but get out of her car and walk to the Caddy and say to the driver, "Hey, you okay? Need any help?"

"You drive like a maniac, lady," was all that the guy behind the wheel could think to say as he shook his head to clear it.

"My driving throw you off?" said Morgan, with a look of distress on her face. "I'm terribly sorry. I just bought my car and was trying to find out what it could do. I thought the streets were deserted here. I guess I didn't see you."

"I was right behind you," said the man.

"You're absolutely right," said Morgan, "I'm completely to blame. If you just give me your name and car registration, I'll make sure my insurance company takes care of all the damage and personal injury."

The man's reaction was instant.

"You've done enough, lady," he said. "Just beat it before you cause any more damage."

"But at least let me take you to a garage," said Morgan.

"I said, beat it!" growled the man. "I'm beginning to get mad, and when I get mad, you don't want to be around me."

"*Well*, if *that's* your attitude, I *don't* want to help you," Morgan said with a show of proper indignation.

"Women drivers," muttered the man.

"Sexist," Morgan said, and stalked back to her car.

As she drove away she saw him standing by his car, surveying his predicament. The look on his face told her he was worried about more than the wreck. He had to be wondering how he could explain his foul-up to Yang.

One thing he wouldn't be able to say was that Morgan suspected anything was wrong. That part of her manoeuver had worked perfectly too.

In fact, she had done more than throw Yang off the track. She had taken another step forward on his trial.

She took a notepad from her shoulder bag and jotted down the number of the Caddy's licence plate.

A New York City licence plate.

She remembered a New York police inspector she knew. His name was Patrick O'Connor. She had met him on a visit to New York the year before, when she had brought him a pickpocket who had made the mistake of trying to loot her shoulder bag. The thief had wound up with a badly sprained arm, and Morgan wound up having dinner with O'Connor. He had urged her to call on him if she ever needed him for anything. She would take him up on that now.

But first she had work to do on her own.

She hit the top of the speed limit on her way back to her apartment. As soon as she opened her apartment door, both her cats came at her, meowing loudly.

Morgan didn't blame them.

"Forgot to feed you before I left, huh?" she said, treading carefully to avoid kicking them as they leaped and circled around her on her way to the refrigerator. Twist and Shout had very strong ideas about their rights.

They did not quieten down until their dishes were filled. Morgan left them feasting, their jaws snapping as they wolfed down their food. For the moment, she noted with a smile, they had forgotten how delicate cats were supposed to be.

By the time Morgan had set herself up at her work table, Twist and Shout had finished their meal and were ready to be companionable again.

Companionable – and curious.

They both leaped up on the table, Twist on one side of Morgan's work area and Shout on the other. There they sat, alternately licking

41

themselves and staring at what she was doing. They could count on Morgan doing the most interesting things when she turned on her electronic microscope and took her chemistry kit out of her shoulder bag.

Right now Morgan was opening a small plastic envelope. Working very carefully, she used a pair of delicate tweezers to lift the contents out.

It was the end of one of her fingernails – one of the fingernails that had scraped Yang's wrist. She had snipped it off and put it in the envelope as soon as she had left Yang's centre.

"See, I've declawed myself," Morgan said to her cats.

She put the fingernail chip on a glass slide and slid it under the microscope lens. After peering at it a moment, she pulled it out. With a tiny scalpel, she did a scraping of the nail and put the scrapings on another slide. Then she looked at that slide through the microscope.

"Gang, I'm in luck," she said. "I don't even have to do a chemical analysis. It's as clear as day."

Visible through the microscope were the skin cells belonging to Yang that Morgan had brought home with her. Just as visible was the clean line between those cells and the substance coating them. Morgan could have done further testing to find out exactly what the substance was, but she didn't have to. She had already seen enough.

"I was right. Yang does dye his skin. I figured his features simply didn't look Oriental enough, British mother or not," she said, as much to herself as to the cats. "That's one more discovery – and one more mystery." She looked first at Twist and then at Shout, who both continued to regard her unblinkingly. "I bet you'd like to be involved with this case, cats. It's like playing with a ball of yarn that keeps on growing bigger the more you unravel it. The only trouble is, this isn't play. I'm getting a stronger and stronger hunch that something serious is going on."

Again she examined the skin cells through her microscope, turning it up to its highest power of magnification. She found what she was looking for. "Bingo! A hair root!" she said. "And it's red! Yang not only shaves his head, he shaves his arms – all the way down to his fingers! I have to hand it to the guy, he certainly is thorough."

When Morgan called New York to speak with Police Inspector Patrick O'Connor a few minutes later, she found out just how thorough Yang was.

"I can check out that licence number while you're waiting," O'Connor told her. "It's on computer. I'll just punch it in." Then, after a pause, he said. "Sorry, but it's a dead end. The plate comes from a car that was stolen, then found abandoned with its plates missing. Anything else I can help you with?"

"You wouldn't by any chance have heard of a guy who calls himself a teacher of higher consciousness? A guy who calls himself Yang?" asked Morgan.

"It doesn't ring a bell," said O'Connor. "I can check it out, though, if you want me to."

"Don't bother," said Morgan. "I'm pretty

sure this Yang just came into being when he arrived here in Langford. But maybe you know of a seven-foot-tall, redheaded crook who operated in New York and then disappeared?"

"I'm afraid that's another strikeout," said O'Connor. "Can you give me a fuller description? A photo, maybe?"

"I don't have one – but I can try to get one," said Morgan. "It would have to be retouched, though. He's wearing a pretty heavy disguise at the moment."

"That's okay," said O'Connor. "We've got artists on the force who are experts at dealing with disguises. Actually, we don't even need a photo. All you have to do is come to New York and work with one of our artists. If you tell him what this Yang looks like, feature by feature, he'll draw a perfect portrait of him. Why not do that, Morgan? I'd like to see you again, anyway. We can have another dinner together and go out on the town."

"That's a pretty roundabout way to ask a girl for a date," said Morgan, grinning into the phone.

"I believe in mixing pleasure with business," said O'Connor. "How about it? When can you get here?"

"Not until next Saturday," said Morgan. "I've got to teach my classes all week."

"Saturday is fine," said O'Connor. "I'm on the day shift that day. We can take care of business – and still have Saturday night free."

"It's a date," said Morgan.

"Great," said O'Connor.

"One thing, though," said Morgan.

"What's that?" said O'Connor.

"I may bring a couple of my students with me."

"Oh?" O'Connor did not sound overjoyed.

"They've had more exposure to Yang than I have," said Morgan. "They can help us put together an accurate picture of him."

"Why not just go get another look at Yang yourself?" suggested O'Connor. "Why get kids invloved?"

"I'm afraid kids are very much involved in this case, whether we like it or not," said Morgan. "Besides, I don't want to make Yang any more suspicious of me than he already is. This guy is definitely sharp. It just took one visit from me to put him on his guard. I don't want to push my luck with another."

"I can see your point," said O'Connor. "Okay, the kids come – and there goes our date."

"Not really," said Morgan. "I strongly doubt the kids will be keen on going out with a couple of old folks like us."

"I know a new club where the action doesn't start until midnight," said O'Connor.

"Sounds good," said Morgan. "See you in a week."

"Can't wait," said O'Connor.

"Neither can I," Morgan said.

Chapter 8

It turned out that Morgan didn't have to wait a full week before she had another piece of the puzzle that was Yang – another piece she had to try to fit into a picture that kept growing more menacing.

Four days later, on Wednesday, Jenny brought it to her.

Morgan knew something was wrong as soon as Jenny came into the chemistry lab that afternoon.

Morgan wasted no time in drawing Jenny aside and asking, "Where's your lab partner? I've never seen you show up here without Sally before."

Jenny's face wore the stiff-lipped expression of someone who had been slapped but was determined not to show any pain.

"Sally isn't my lab partner anymore," Jenny said. "She told me this morning. She said that Amy Parsons needed a lab partner, and asked her, and Sally said yes."

"Kind of sudden, isn't it?" asked Morgan. "Not to mention strange."

"Actually, I was expecting it," said Jenny.

"Since when?" asked Morgan.

"Since Saturday," said Jenny. "Saturday afternoon."

"What happened then?"

"She was chosen by Yang," said Jenny with a

46

grimace, as if she were tasting something bitter.

"Chosen for what?" asked Morgan, suddenly extra alert.

"To be advanced," said Jenny, clearly as eager to tell someone about it as Morgan was to listen. "Yang yanked her out of the beginners' class we both were in, and he put her in the special advanced class that only Amy and Carl and Sam were in. He said he could see her consciousness was already at a level where it could benefit from more rewarding training."

"And not you?" said Morgan.

"And not me," said Jenny with another grimace. "I think it was because I made Yang mad."

"How?"

"I spoke to him in Chinese, you know, to show him I could speak his language," Jenny said. "I guess I was kind of trying to show off for him. But he didn't understand a word I said. He claimed it was because his father came from a different region in China, where they spoke a different dialect. I didn't tell him that I was speaking Mandarin, which practically all educated people speak all over China, but even without me giving him any back talk, I could see he didn't like the idea of a student knowing more about anything than he did. Not many grownups do, I guess. But I thought Yang was different."

"And did Sally do anything special to rate his approval?" asked Morgan.

Jenny shook her head. "Nothing I could see. That's what made it so strange. I mean, I know Sally real well, better than practically anyone, and I didn't see any signs of the higher consciousness that Yang said he saw."

"Think hard," said Morgan. "Was there anything Yang could have noticed? Something Sally did or said? Try to remember. It could be important."

Jenny's brow furrowed. Again she shook her head. "Nothing." Then her head stopped shaking. "Except one thing, maybe."

"What was that?" asked Morgan.

"It was you," said Jenny.

"*Me?*"

"When Sally and I were coming down the street to go to our class at the centre, we saw you leave, get into your car, and drive away. When we arrived, Sally asked Yang what you were doing there. She said she was hoping you would start going to the centre too, since you were her favourite teacher."

"And Yang seemed interested in that?" Morgan said.

"Just for a minute – then he seemed to forget all about it," said Jenny. "But then an hour later, Sally got promoted – and I got left behind."

"And when did Sally start attending the advanced class?" asked Morgan.

"On Monday," Jenny said. "That's all I can tell you. I thought I'd hear all about it from Sally, but when I called her up that night, it was the shortest phone conversation on record. She said she wasn't supposed to talk about the class, because that would interfere with the learning process. I didn't ask her any more about it, because I could hear she didn't even *want* to talk about it. In fact, I could hear she didn't want to talk to me about *anything*. And that's the last time she did talk to me, except to tell me we weren't lab partners anymore. If you want to find out anything else about Sally or about Yang, you'll have to ask Sally herself. Because I'm not going to have anything more to do with her, and I'm not going back to Yang's, either."

"Look, do me a favour, Jenny," Morgan said. "Keep on going to Yang's a little while longer. I want to find out as much as I can about what's going on there."

"Okay, just for you," said Jenny, not looking happy about the idea.

"I'll even give you a reward for you investigation," said Morgan. "A free trip to New York this weekend – and a chance to take part in a real-life game of cops and robbers. We have to find out what Yang is stealing. I'm pretty sure he *is* stealing something. Sally, for one thing. We have to find a way to get her back."

"*Okay*," said Jenny, perking up.

Then, suddenly, she shut up and looked away.

Sally had just arrived in the lab, with Amy. With them were Carl and Sam, another pair of lab partners. Together they formed a tight little group of four.

Jenny kept as far away from them as she could, working by herself. She kept her attention strictly on her work, carefully not even glancing in their direction.

Meanwhile, Morgan spent the lab period trying to figure out the best way to get Sally off by herself to quiz her. But Sally saved her the trouble. Right after the lab, she split away from the group and came over to Morgan.

"I know you want to find out as much as you can about Yang's centre, " said Sally, smiling brightly. "And I think I can tell you all you want to know."

Morgan looked at her closely as she spoke. Sally's eyes were as bright as her smile, telling Morgan nothing.

"Thanks," said Morgan. "I do admit I'm sort of curious."

"Maybe this isn't the best place to talk, though," said Sally. "Maybe we can go someplace private – like your flat."

"Whatever you say," said Morgan, not showing the slight surprise she felt at this suggestion. Students might think of her more as a friend than a teacher, but none had ever suggested making a social call before. Maybe this release from restraint was part of the higher consciousness that Yang produced. Maybe his message came straight from the sixties: *Let it all hang out*.

Certainly Sally made no attempt to hide her curiosity when they arrived at Morgan's.

"Gee, this place is super-cool," she said, looking around as though she'd never been there before. She stared at the autographed Police poster. "Hey, rumour has it that you actually had a *thing* going with Sting. Any truth to that?"

"Sad to say, not much," said Morgan with a mock look of regret. "The Police were having a concert in San Francisco a few years ago, and they needed a techie in a hurry when their

50

sound system broke down. I just happened to be able to do the job. I mean, Sting and I had coffee together a few times, but it never went any further than that – except for the funny postcards he sends me now and then from some of the weird places that he visits when he's touring."

"But I can tell you must have been into the rock scene," said Sally. "I mean that silver streak in your hair is a dead giveaway. Definitely hip. You make all the other teachers look like they're right out of the Stone Age. One thing for sure, they're not part of the stoned age. I bet you know that scene too."

"Not really," said Morgan. "I may teach about chemicals, but I don't get high from them."

"Come on," said Sally. "Not even a little? Now and then?"

"Not even a little," said Morgan. "I like to get high without help, just like I'd rather run on my own legs than have someone carry me. I'm afraid I'm just a freak for doing things the natural way – and that goes for my hair. That silver streak is my own."

"You mean you were *born* with it?" asked Sally.

"No," said Morgan. "It appeared a couple of years ago, overnight, after –" Morgan paused, then finished her sentence brusquely. "After an accident I was in."

Sally was not put off by Morgan's clear reluctance to discuss the matter. "What kind of accident?" she asked immediately.

"A car accident," said Morgan, in the same

curt tone.

"You get hurt?" asked Sally.

"Not a scratch," said Morgan.

"Anyone else involved?" Sally pursued. "Another car? Or maybe somebody in your car?"

"Look, Sally," said Morgan. "It's kind of a painful memory. I'd just as soon not go into it. It's like opening an old wound."

"Sure, I understand," said Sally. But her words were automatic, devoid of any real apology. Already she was moving on to the next object of her curiosity.

She was looking at the portrait of the Renaissance prince that hung on Morgan's wall. "What a great-looking guy. It's a shame they don't make many dreamboats like him anymore."

"Yeah, it's a shame," said Morgan in a very quiet voice, as if something had got into her throat.

Sally looked at Morgan hard, then said, "You know, I bet that prince in the picture reminds you of somebody."

"Look, Sally, I don't like to sound like a shrinking violet, but there are some things I'd rather not –"

But Sally wasn't about to be stopped. Her eyes were intent, her voice intense. "Sure, that must be why you don't go steady with any guy. I mean, there are rumours around school that you don't really like guys very much, but I never figured they were true. The way I see it, you must be in love with some guy, some guy who isn't here, some guy who looks like that guy in the painting . . ." Sally's voice trailed off in speculation. Then it came back strong. "Maybe that guy was hurt in that accident you were in. Maybe even worse than hurt. Maybe even –"

"Sally, I think this has gone far enough," Morgan said, and her voice was loud now, louder even than she intended.

It was loud enough to get through to Sally at last. Sally blinked and stopped looking around her. Her eyes suddenly seemed to have lost their focus. For a moment Sally did not seem to know where she was.

"To get back to your reason for being here," Morgan said. "You were going to tell me what you found out about Yang."

"Oh, yeah, sure, that's right," Sally said vaguely.

"I understand you're in one of his advanced classes, with Amy and Carl and Sam," Morgan prompted her.

"Right, yeah, right," said Sally.

"And what did you find out?" Morgan continued to press her.

"Oh, the class is real nice and all," said Sally. Her voice had the sound of someone reciting a speech learned by heart. "We do these meditations and we clear our minds and we release all our energies. I've just begun the class and I can already feel how much easier my schoolwork is and how much more confident I am about how I look when I audition for a modelling job. I've even made a good beginning at getting rid of this fear I've always had that when I do baton twirling, I'll make a gruesome slip. Amy and Carl and Sam say they've all had the same kind

53

of great experience. That's why they all hang out together, and that's why I've started hanging out with them too. I mean, other people simply can't understand how great it feels to have all that inner power to command. Why, I can see by the way you're looking at me that even you don't understand."

Morgan nodded. "You're right, Sally. I don't understand. Not completely. Not yet. But believe me, I mean to try."

Chapter 9

Morgan and Jenny watched Yang's face emerge piece by piece.

They sat in a fluorescent-lit room in a lower Manhattan police precinct headquarters. With them were Police Inspector Patrick O'Connor and Tony Angelo, a police department artist.

Angelo worked with a soft drawing pencil and with extraordinary speed, dashing off one sketch after another. First he drew the shape of a head. Then he asked Jenny and Morgan whether Yang's head was longer or shorter, wider or narrower, than the one on the paper. Following Morgan's and Jenny's directions, he drew a series of heads that came closer and closer to Yang's, until he had the exact shape on paper.

Then he followed the same procedure when drawing Yang's features – ears, nose, eyes, mouth, chin, cheekbones – until the floor was littered with abandoned sketches and Yang's face was on the piece of paper on the table.

"That's him," said Morgan.

"It sure is," agreed Jenny.

"Now could you make him a redhead?" Morgan said to the artist.

Angelo nodded. With a coloured pencil he gave Yang red hair, and with another pencil he gave Yang the pale complexion that redheads usually had.

"So that's what he looks like," said Jenny

wonderingly. "I don't think I'd recognize him looking like that."

"It's amazing how a different skin colour changes people's perceptions of someone," said Morgan. "Yang really knew what he was doing when he disguised himself. But now that we've removed that disguise, maybe we can find out what else he's doing – and what he's done." She turned to O'Connor. "Is he a crook? Do you recognize him?"

"Nope," said O'Connor, shaking his head slowly, unwillingly. "Before you got here, I went through our file on con men to refresh my memory. I didn't see this face. And I didn't find any mention of anyone almost seven feet tall." But O'Connor kept staring at Yang's picture. "The thing is, though, I keep feeling that I have seen that face before. But I can't remember when or where. It's maddening – like an itch I can't reach to scratch."

"What about that fingerprint I sent to you?" asked Morgan.

It had been Jenny who had got that fingerprint, all on her own, by picking up a teacup that she saw Yang using at the centre. She brought it to Morgan, who used fingerprint powder to make the print visible, then photographed it and sent it Express Mail to O'Connor. As a bonus discovery, Morgan had analyzed the remains of the "tea" in the cup and found out it was brandy.

"Another dead end," said O'Connor. "I did a computer check on it. We don't have it in our files. I even sent it to the F.B.I. central computer in Washington. No soap there, either."

"This hasn't been one of my more successful hunting expeditions," said Morgan. She shrugged. "I'll have to figure out a different approach when I get back to Langford. I don't know much about this Yang yet, but I know enough to know that whatever he's doing to those kids, it has to be stopped – fast."

"I hope you'll take off enough time for our date tonight," said O'Connor. "It doesn't make much sense for you to go back to Massachusetts right away. Besides, we might come up with some interesting ideas about the case together."

"And don't forget, you're supposed to take me to the Museum of Natural History this afternoon," said Jenny. "My parents will ask me about it when I get home. This supposed to be an educational trip, remember?"

"Okay, our date is still on, Pat," said Morgan. "And I'll give you a quick tour of the town this afternoon, Jenny, though it's a tough place to visit. To know it, you really have to live here."

"Did you?" asked Jenny.

"Just for a summer, when I took a graduate course at Columbia," said Morgan. "But it was enough to let me learn how much a tourist never sees. Maybe someday you'll get a chance to see *that* New York too. Right now, though, you'll have to settle for the high points."

Once Morgan and Jenny were outside police headquarters, looking at the twin towers of the World Trade Center, it was easy to decide what the first high point would be.

Morgan glanced at her watch. "It's just one o'clock. We'll have time to whiz up to the top, take a quick look, and whiz down. After that, we'll head uptown to some of the museums."

The high-speed elevator to the top of the tower left Jenny's ears ringing. Her eyes were left blinking as she looked out at the city spread below her, the entire island of Manhattan, bordered by twin rivers and jammed with buildings.

"It looks like a huge city built by ants," she said.

But she forgot about the fantastic view when she heard Morgan whisper close to her ear, "Don't make any obvious movement of your head, but take a sideways look at those guys standing at the railing about ten feet to our left. Tell me if you recognize either of them."

Jenny did as asked. She saw the guys that Morgan was talking about. One of them was tall, with a full beard and mirrored sunglasses. The other was short and thin, with a clean-shaven, hatchet-jawed face and a blond crew cut. Both of them wore cheap brown wash-and-wear suits.

"I don't know the big guy, though there is something familiar about him," Jenny said under her breath to Morgan while looking straight ahead her. "But the short guy, wasn't he on the plane we took to New York last night?"

"He must have been following us," said Morgan. "And I have a good idea who his boss is."

"You know the other one?" asked Jenny, feeling her heart begin to beat faster.

"He was driving a car that trailed me last week – just after I left Yang's," said Morgan.

"What do you think they mean to do?" asked Jenny.

"I don't know – and I don't want to stick around to find out," said Morgan. "Let's head for the elevator. But walk slowly. We don't want to let them know we're on to them."

At a leisurely pace Jenny walked with Morgan toward the long bank of elevators. Out of the corner of her eye she saw the two men leave the railing and follow in their trail.

"Keep on walking – slowly," Morgan said, "until you see one of the elevators beginning to close its doors. Then we'll make a dash for it."

Morgan's strategy worked – almost.

They saw an elevator closing – and raced to shove themselves abroad, with the two men still ten feet away.

They would have been zooming downward, leaving the men hundreds of floors behind, if a good samaritan among their fellow passengers hadn't spotted the men breaking into a run to get abroad, and held the door open so they could make it.

"Must be a tourist," muttered Morgan as the two men squeezed themselves aboard. Then there was only the unearthly hum of the elevator as it dropped downward. Jenny's heart was in her throat by the time they reached the ground floor, and not just because of the speed of the descent. The two men got out first and paused by the door as Jenny and Morgan passed them by. Then their trailing resumed.

"What now?" Jenny whispered as they stood before the revolving doors that led out of the building.

"We have to keep going down," said Morgan. "As soon as we get outside, we'll make a run for the subway entrance on the corner. Maybe we can get down the subway stairs before those guys get out of the building."

A minute later they were down the stairs and racing along a graffiti-covered, white-tiled underground corridor that led to the trains. Jenny could sense Morgan holding back so that Jenny could keep up with her as they tore past men, women and children who seemed to find nothing strange in the sight of two people doing a hundred-yard dash in the BMT. Jenny hadn't been in New York long, but she already had a suspicion that nothing less than a nuclear attack would make the natives lose their cool.

Jenny was gasping when they reached the subway token booth.

But she had plenty of time to catch her breath.

The token booth attendant was explaining to a man standing in front of them how he could reach a stop in Brooklyn. The traveller spoke broken English with a heavy Russian accent. The attendant spoke fluent English with a heavy Spanish accent. By the time the attendant explained that the man would have to take a B train, then tranfer to an RR, and then to a D express, Jenny had her breath back – but she wasn't breathing any easier.

The two men were back on their trail and coming right for them.

Morgan saw them too.

"Two tokens, quick," she said, shoving a

couple of dollar bills toward the attendant. *"Please."*

The attendant responded to the urgency in her voice by saying, "What's the rush? Don't be in such a hurry. You'll live longer."

"That's what you think," Morgan muttered, her voice drowned out by the mounting roar of an approaching train.

The attendant examined the bills as if trying to memorize the serial numbers. He slid the tokens towards Morgan as if moving them over treacle. He began the same laborious process with the two dimes he owed them.

"Keep the change, live it up," said Morgan, grabbing the tokens.

On the run she led Jenny through the turnstiles towards the waiting train.

"We're in luck," Jenny said as they squeezed themselves through the closing subway doors.

Through the grime-streaked window Jenny saw the two men coming through the turnstiles. But they could only stop and glare helplessly at the closed doors of the train. Jenny relaxed as the train lurched into motion.

Then, abruptly, the train shuddered to a standstill.

And the passengers packed aboard began to groan.

"Oh, *no*."

"Not *again*."

"And I've got a doctor's appointment."

"That's nothing. I've got a job interview."

"You think that's bad – I'm going to my own wedding."

Morgan explained to Jenny what Jenny could

already guess. "When you take a New York subway, you're *never* in luck. In fact, luck is what you need."

Through the window Jenny saw the angry frustration on the men's faces change to smiling eagerness. Then the subway doors slid open and a voice that sounded like Donald Duck came over the train's loudspeaker system: "Passengers will all leave this train. This train is being taken out of service. We are very sorry for this inconvenience."

"Not as sorry as we are," Morgan said as she and Jenny were swept up by the flood of people pouring out of the train.

Helplessly they were shoved toward the men who were moving to meet them now, closing in, to make sure Morgan and Jenny would not escape this time.

Chapter 10

"What happened? Where are we?" groaned Jenny as she opened her eyes.

She saw that she and Morgan were in a brightly lit, windowless, pearl-grey room.

She looked at Morgan, who was sitting with her back propped up against the wall, and saw that Morgan was unconscious.

Then Jenny began to remember.

She remembered being swept out of the subway car with Morgan and seeing the two men closing in on them.

She remembered thinking that at least for the moment they were safe here on the subway platform, among all these people.

She remembered one of the two men, the shorter one, moving next to her, pressing against her.

She remembered a sudden, stinging sensation.

After that, everything faded.

All she could recall were voices that came from far away.

"They've fainted."

"Don't crowd them. Give them air."

"They should sue the city."

Then a man's voice, louder than the others, close to her ear: "We'll take care of them. We're doctors."

Then she remembered – nothing.

That was all she knew – except that she needed help.

"Wake up, *please*," she said to Morgan.

Jenny sighed with relief as Morgan's eyelids fluttered open. Within seconds, as Jenny watched, Morgan's eyes focused. Jenny could practically hear Morgan's mind humming into action.

"That was a heavy drug they knocked us out with, but it doesn't seem to have left any bad effects," said Morgan. She looked at her arm. "They must have used an advanced-model hypodermic. It was fast and barely made a mark."

"But how could those two guys get away with it?" said Jenny. "I mean, just carry us off that way, in front of everyone."

"I'm sure the crowd must have applauded them," said Morgan. "In this city everyone is happy to let somebody else take care of anyone in trouble. Not only does it save people from having to miss appointments, it also protects them from lawsuits in case the injured party doesn't feel well enough taken care of. All those two guys had to do was volunteer to take responsibility for us and they had us right where they wanted us – in their hands."

"I guess that's where we are, all right," said Jenny. "But where?"

Morgan rose to her feet and began to inspect the room.

"Not many clues," she said, looking at the blank walls, the bare floor. Then she reached the door. "Now, *this* is interesting."

Jenny joined her in looking at the door. It *was*

interesting, on three counts.

It wasn't wood but metal, and it was painted the same pearl-grey as the rest of the room.

It had no doorknob, no handle, not even a keyhole.

And at its centre was one tiny, round glass spy hole. When Jenny peered into it, she saw only the reflection of her own eye.

"This is a one-way mirror," said Morgan. "We can't look out through it, but somebody on the outside can look in on us."

Morgan gazed at the door a moment longer, then went on, "There are only two kinds of places I know that use doors like this. One is a prison – and I think we can rule that out. And the other is a hospital for the mentally ill."

"An insane asylum? said Jenny.

"As crazy as it sounds," said Morgan, nodding. "But it really isn't that surprising. This whole case is getting crazier and crazier."

Then her voice dropped to an urgent whisper. "Quick, press against the wall, next to me."

Jenny heard the same thing Morgan had. On the other side of the door, someone was turning a key in the lock.

Jenny saw Morgan's strategy instantly. When the door was opened and swung inward, Morgan and she would be concealed behind it, in a good spot to spring out and dash past whoever entered.

Standing pressed against the wall beside Morgan, she tensed herself.

Then a voice came through a hidden speaker system into the room. It was a woman's voice, gentle, soothing, slightly amused: "Now, let's not play any games, girls. We can see you, you know – the entire room is monitored by TV. Now, please go to the other side of the room, as far from the door as possible, so that you won't be tempted to do anything foolish when I come in."

"Come on, Jenny," said Morgan, following the voice's orders and going to the other side of the room.

"At least we'll find out what's going on here, and who's in charge."

Jenny followed and stood watching as the door swung open.

The woman who entered could have posed for a picture of the Angel of Mercy. She had snowy-white hair, a kindly, slightly lined face and a crisp, spotless white nurse's uniform. Of medium height, she was dwarfed by the burly male attendant in white who entered with her.

"What are we doing here? We demand to be let out," Morgan said as soon as the nurse and the attendant were in the room.

"Please don't excite youself. It's not good for you," the nurse said soothingly.

"You'd be excited too if a couple of strange guys drugged you and locked you up," Morgan said.

"Of course I would," said the nurse, giving an almost imperceptible nod to the attendant.

"You don't believe me, do you?" said Morgan.

"Of course I do," said the nurse. "I'm sure that's exactly what you think happened."

"It *did* happen," said Jenny. "A couple of guys chased us down from the top of the World

Trade Center and trapped us in the subway and stuck needles in our arms."

"You both believe the same thing," said the nurse. "The doctors were right. This is a most unusual case. No wonder they wanted you isolated."

"We're telling the truth! We're *not* crazy," insisted Jenny, her voice angry. Too late she saw Morgan making signs with her hand for Jenny to cool it.

Jenny's anger had made up the nurse's mind.

"Of course you're not crazy," she said. "But you are getting a bit too excited."

The nurse nodded at the attendant again, and they both moved toward Jenny and Morgan. When they were halfway across the room, they both reached into their pockets and pulled out hypodermics.

"Look, you don't have to do that," said Morgan in a calm, reasonable voice. "Honest."

"It's for your own good," answered the nurse, just as calmly and reasonably. Then, as the attendant grabbed Morgan, her hand moved swiftly to seize Jenny's arm. For an elderly looking woman, she had a grip like an iron clamp. Struggling helplessly, Jenny saw the nurse's other hand targeting the hypodermic at her arm. It was all happening fast, yet it seemed like a film in slow motion or a scream of fear that lasted forever.

There was a scream. Not from Jenny – but from Morgan.

Time seemed to freeze. The nurse froze. The attendant who held Morgan by one arm froze. And Morgan stopped screaming and started falling toward the ground in a dead faint.

Instinctively the attendant dropped the hypodermic he was holding to catch Morgan in both hands – and that was all Morgan needed to stop falling and start moving.

With a burst of strength, she broke free of the unprepared attendant's grip. In the next instant the hypodermic was in her hand, and in the attendant's arm.

"Stop! You can't –" the nurse began.

She didn't get to finish the sentence. Morgan already had the nurse's arm twisted behind the nurse, and then the nurse's hypodermic in the nurse's arm. A moment later the nurse joined the attendant lying unconscious on the floor.

"Surprise is a wonderful weapon," said Morgan, looking down at them. "My martial arts master used to tell me it beats all other methods of overcoming stronger adversaries." Then Morgan grinned. "But this is no time for a lecture. Let's get out of here – fast."

They went out through the open door and entered a corridor with another door at the far end, fifteen feet away.

They moved toward it.

"Let's hope it isn't locked," said Morgan.

It wasn't. It opened easily – before Morgan or Jenny touched it.

Standing in the doorway facing them were the two men who had brought them here. This time they did not have hypodermics in their hands. They had pistols.

"That was quite a show you put on in the room back there," said the tall, bearded man. "We got back to this place just in time to

68

catch it on TV."

"We're real sorry you didn't want the shots that the nice nurse had for you," said the other man. His face split into a big grin. "Maybe you'll like our shots better. They'll *really* put you to sleep – for good."

Chapter 11

"You'll never get away with this," said Morgan, refusing to flinch at the pistols and looking straight at the bearded man. "You can't just gun us down and get away with it."

"Gun you down?" said the bearded man. "We wouldn't dream of it – unless you make us."

"Bullets are so crude," said his partner. "We're not clods, you know. We're experts."

"Experts at what?" asked Morgan.

"You'll see," said the bearded man.

"Soon," said his partner. He motioned with his gun. "Let's get back to your room."

The nurse and the attendant were still lying there unconscious. The bearded man gave them a quick glance.

"They'll be out for hours," he said.

"That'll give us plenty of time," said his partner.

"Let's not waste it," said the bearded man.

They didn't. Within ten minutes they had Morgan and Jenny tied up hand and foot.

The bearded man left the room. When he returned, he held another hypodermic. This one was old-fashioned, with a large plunger and a long needle. Jenny could see that it was filled with a cloudy liquid.

"I'm surprised at you, Miss Swift," the bearded man said. "Taking a student to the big city and introducing her to drugs."

"Of course, it isn't really surprising," said his partner. "Everyone at your school knows you're weird."

"But you should have been more careful," said the bearded man. "The stuff you injected was so strong to handle. And dying of an overdose is such a nasty way to go."

"Still, it happens all the time," said his partner. "The cops who find your bodies will know exactly what happened. Just two more O.D.'s"

Morgan tried to think of something to say, to do. She could only turn to Jenny and say, "I'm sorry for getting you into this."

"That's okay – it's not your fault," Jenny said, trying not to sound scared so that she wouldn't make Morgan feel even worse.

"That's right – it's just your funeral," said the bearded man. He raised his hypodermic to plunge it into Morgan's arm.

Jenny shut her eyes to keep from screaming.

A shouting voice opened them.

"Drop it – and freeze."

Jenny saw the bearded man drop his hypodermic, and his partner drop his gun. Both raised their empty hands high above their heads.

"No girl runs out on a date with me – no matter how far I have to go to hunt her down," said Patrick O'Connor. He untied Morgan while three other policemen kept their guns on the bearded man and his partner.

On the ride downtown to the police station, O'Connor explained what had happened.

"A guy on the subway platform spotted the needle being shoved into Jenny's arm. He didn't do anything at the time – he was late to a concert, and beside, he makes it a rule never to get involved in other people's affairs. But he kept thinking about it, and during intermission he called up the police. Nobody could make any sense of his story, until I went to pick you up for our date and you weren't there, and I put two and two together. After that, it was just a matter of finding the driver of the cab those guys used to take you to the hospital, and getting there as fast as I could."

"You mean, it was a real hospital?" said Morgan.

"Sure was," said O'Connor. "A very private hospital for very rich people, right on Park Avenue."

"Those two guys – they weren't real doctors, were they?" asked Jenny.

"That's what I have to find out," said O'Connor.

Two hours later he came out of the interrogation room to tell Morgan and Jenny, "I didn't find out much. Those two are doctors, all right. Psychologists. They showed me their credentials and I checked them out. But when I asked them what they were doing with you, they clammed up. I mean, totally clammed up. I never saw anything like it. It was like they went into a kind of trance as soon as I mentioned you. And the same thing happened when I asked them about that Yang guy you think is their boss."

"He is their boss," said Morgan. "I'm sure of it."

"I believe you," said O'Connor. "But nobody else will. You need proof. Not to mention some idea of what he's up to."

"That's what I mean to find out," said Morgan. "If he was willing to kill Jenny and me, I hate to think what he wants to do with those kids he has believing he's the source of all wisdom and power."

"And I want to help you," said Jenny. "I get a chill when I think of Amy and Carl and Sam and Sally."

"If I could just remember where I saw Yang's face before," said O'Connor. He shook his head. "It's there, somewhere in my brain, but I can't seem to reach it."

"Call me up if you do," said Morgan. "Right now, I have to get back to Langford. That's where Yang is, and that's where I want to be – right in the path of whatever he's planning to do. I have a strong feeling that time is running out." She paused and looked at her digital watch. "My God, it's Sunday already. We were knocked out for over twenty-four hours. Come on, Jenny, we have a plane to catch."

They barely caught it, charging up the steps to leap through the door of the lone daily plane to Langford just as the boarding ramp was about to be rolled away.

They landed at the Langford airport as the sun was setting.

"You know something, Jenny," said Morgan as they climbed into her Mercedes 190 in the parking lot. "All this action yesterday has made me forget something very important."

"What's that?" asked Jenny.

"I've forgotten to eat," said Morgan. "I'm *starving*."

"You know something?" said Jenny.

"What?"

"So am I," Jenny said. She wasn't kidding. She could practically hear her own stomach rumbling above the roar of the car engine.

"As my Zen master always told me, 'Eat when hungry'," Morgan said. "Want to join me for a pizza? With the works. We can pick it up and eat it at my place while we discuss strategy. As an old saying that I just made up goes, you can't fight evil on an empty stomach."

"Sounds as good as any of those sayings of Confucius my parents are constantly feeding me," said Jenny. "Especially if you go heavy on the pepperoni."

The huge pizza that the counterman put in a carton for them was mouth-watering.

"I'll try not to break any speeding laws – but I make no promises," said Morgan as she headed the car home.

She led Jenny up to her floor two steps at a time. She put the key into her lock, tried to turn it, and said quietly, "That's funny, it's unlocked."

She put her ear to the door.

Her voice dropped to a whisper. "Someone's in there."

"Should we call the cops?" Jenny whispered back.

"It's more important to find out who it is," Morgan said. "We can't give the prowler time to get away. I'm going in. Keep a safe distance behind me."

74

"But you don't have a weapon," Jenny said.

"That's what you think," said Morgan, swinging the door open very slowly, very silently.

The only light in the room was the beam of a flashlight playing over Morgan's desk. The person holding the flashlight was only a shadowy shape bent over the desk.

Morgan moved faster than Jenny thought anyone could move – like a bolt of dark lightning.

She was behind the intruder almost before her steps sounded in the still room.

As the intruder turned, with the flashlight blazing into Morgan's face, Morgan didn't blink. She just slammed the steaming pizza she had whipped out of the carton into the intruder's face.

The surprise was total – but it was nothing compared to the shock Jenny got when Morgan snatched the flashlight up from the floor and shone it directly at the intruder, who was using both hands to pull the sticky mess away.

"It can't be! said Jenny.

But it was.

"Hi, Sally," said Morgan.

Chapter 12

Morgan saw the dazed look on Sally's pizza-streaked face and said, "Before I start asking questions, why don't you wash up, Sally?"

Sally blinked, as if Morgan's words were in a foreign tongue. Then she slowly nodded. She went into the bathroom. When she came back, her face was clean, but her eyes were still clouded.

"What am I doing here?" she asked.

"You don't *know*? Come *on*," said Jenny, looking at her best friend and seeing a stranger, someone who broke into flats to do – what?

"I tell you, I *don't* know," Sally said, with a plea for understanding in her voice. "Please believe me."

"Of course we believe you," said Morgan, putting a comforting hand on Sally's shoulder.

"Sure we do," said Jenny, and the warmth in her voice said that Sally was still her best friend.

"But what *was* I doing here?" said Sally. "I should know. I want to know."

"We all want to know," said Morgan. "And we can find out – if you cooperate."

"I'll do anything you want," said Sally. "Anything I *can*, anyway. My mind feels so funny – like it's a wheel spinning in empty air."

"Let's use deductive reasoning," said Morgan. "We'll start with what we saw you doing here – and try to figure out why you were doing it. You were searching my desk with a flashlight, looking for something. But what?"

"No idea," Sally said with pained helplessness. "I don't even remember coming here tonight".

"I remember the last time you came here," said Morgan. "You had a lot of questions about me and my past and my private life – questions I didn't choose to answer. Maybe you were looking for the answers tonight."

"The last time I was here? Questions about your private life?" Sally grew even more confused. "When was that?"

"*Think*," Jenny urged her, then wished she hadn't.

By now Sally was close to tears. "I *can't*. I don't remember. I must be losing my mind."

"Relax," said Morgan softly. "You're not losing your mind. Something has happened to it, though. Look, would you mind telling me in detail what goes on in Yang's advanced class?"

"I'm not supposed to," said Sally. "He made me promise."

"Sally," Jenny said. "This is us. Morgan. Me. Your friends."

"You have to help us before we can help you," said Morgan.

"We want to help," said Jenny, and her eyes met Sally's. "That's what friends are for."

Sally bit her lip.

"Well, I guess it can't hurt," she said reluctantly. "I mean, there really isn't much to tell. We really don't do anything big or dramatic. We just practice meditation and mind-emptying exercises, you know, to put us in touch with our vital inmost energies."

"Yang's words, I presume," said Morgan.

"Yeah, right," said Sally.

"And Yang is present when you do those exercises?" Morgan said.

"Of course, always," said Sally. "I mean, he has to be. We need him to lead us, show us the way."

"All of you at once?" asked Morgan.

"No," said Sally. "He says that even at our level we still have to be free from the distractions of other students. He takes us one by one into a separate room."

"And what does he do there?" asked Morgan.

"I don't know about the others, but he has me gaze into a candle that represents the pure light of universal consciousness that my mind must merge with," said Sally.

"And after that?" Morgan pursued.

"That's all that happens," said Sally. "My mind goes totally empty until Yang tells me I've finished my exercise and can go forth refreshed and strengthened."

"Yang's words again?" said Morgan dryly.

"Well, he's right," Sally said with a touch of defensiveness. "Those exercises leave me feeling great, on top of everything. I feel like I can do anything I want – and when I try, it turns out I can. You can't tell me I'm imagining that, just like you can't tell me Yang has anything to do with my weirdness. I mean, I'd know it if he did, wouldn't I?"

"If I knew for sure, I'd tell you," said Morgan.

"Well, *I'm* sure Yang is at the bottom of it,"

said Jenny.

"I hate to say it, Jenny, and I hope you don't take it wrong, but maybe that's because he didn't ask you into his advanced class," said Sally. "I mean, it would be only natural for you to be a little, well, resentful. And there's no way for you to know how much he can do for a person."

"There's no way for you to know what *somebody* tried to do to Morgan and me today," Jenny answered sharply.

Morgan cut her off. "It's not enough for us to have suspicions. In science, that's called having only a hypothesis. We need hard evidence. We have to set up some kind of experiment to give us proof." She turned to Sally. "Look, don't worry about this incident tonight. I'm beginning to get a pretty good idea of what's going on."

"What is it?" asked Jenny eagerly.

"Before I can tell you, I have to find one key piece of the puzzle that's still missing," said Morgan.

"I hope you find it soon," said Sally. "You might have a piece of your puzzle missing – but there's a piece of my mind that I can't find."

"Believe me, I'll do it as fast as I can," said Morgan. "But you'll have to do something too – something you might not want to."

"What?" said Sally.

"Skip your classes with Yang – just for a few days. You can call in sick."

"But –" Sally began.

"You have to do it," said Morgan, and there was no softness in her voice. "Or there's nothing I can do."

"But Yang is sure to –" Sally said.

"It's for your own good," said Morgan. "Trust me. Just for a few days."

"If you say so," said Sally reluctantly.

"I say so," Morgan said, and looked at her watch. "Time for you two to be heading home. You need your sleep and so do I. Tomorrow promises to be busy day."

Chapter 13

Morgan was right.

The next day was busy. Even busier than she expected.

Morgan didn't even have time for lunch. Instead she found herself in the office of the school principal, Mr Marsh. She was summoned by Mr Marsh himself.

Whenever Morgan was face to face with Mr Marsh, she had to keep reminding herself to call him Mr Marsh and not his nickname among almost all the students and many of the teachers.

Mr Marshmallow.

His nickname came only partly from his physical appearance, which was round and soft.

Mainly it came from the firmness of his opinions and decisions, or rather, the lack of it.

If person A told Mr Marshmallow that it was about to rain, he would immediately open his umbrella. If person B told Mr Marshmallow that the sun was about to come out, Mr Marshmallow would not only close his umbrella, he would buy some tanning lotion.

Today Morgan was hearing what Mr Marshmallow had most recently been told.

"This morning I received three different phone calls from parents, Miss Swift," Mr Marshmallow said. "They were all about you."

"Praise, I hope," Morgan said. "I need all the

flattery I can get to supplement my income. Speaking of which, I'd like to talk about a raise for next –"

"This is *not* the time to discuss a raise for you," said Mr Marsh as sharply as he could. The effort to sound stern brought a flush to his pale skin, and beads of sweat to his forehead and bald head. "These parents had harsh words about you, Miss Swift, harsh words indeed."

"Actually, I prefer being called *Ms* Swift," said Morgan. " I thought we already agreed to that."

Mr Marsh cleared his throat. "Well, yes, I know. One forgets these things. I'm sorry if I offended you, Miss, er, *Ms* Swift." He tried to regain his tone of authority. "But back to the original subject. These parents, and there were three of them, had strong complaints about you."

"And what were they?" asked Morgan.

"One parent was concerned about your clothing. He thought it inappropriate for a teacher to wear blue jeans to class one day, a Japanese jumpsuit the next, and a 1920s-style dress the next."

"We went over that last year," said Morgan. "We agreed that if my clothes were clean and not sexually provocative, I had the right to dress to suit the way I felt that day."

"Well, of course, you're right, we did. I merely thought I'd pass on the comment," said Mr Marsh. Then his voice grew firm again. "But the second complaint was more serious. This parent was disturbed by your teaching methods. She said you did not provide a strong

82

enough authority figure and were far too intimate with students."

"I don't think I have to defend my teaching," said Morgan. "I'll let the test marks of my students speak for themselves."

"Yes, yes," said Mr Marsh, by now making soothing gestures with his hands.

"Any more complaints?" assked Morgan.

"Well, there was one," said Mr Marsh. "A parent was annoyed that you seemed to be interfering in his child's after-school life. Something about your quizzing the child about some exercise class the child is going to."

"Do you think it's *wrong* to be interested in a student's welfare?" demanded Morgan.

"Of course not, Ms Swift," said Mr Marsh. "And I want to assure you, the school is absolutely delighted with your work. I just thought we'd touch base on this little matter. I like to maintain a constant contact with my teaching staff. But now I won't take up any more of your valuable –"

"Before I leave I'd like to know the names of the complaining parents," said Morgan.

"I don't really think that's necessary," said Mr Marsh. "We can just forget the entire matter. Let sleeping dogs lie."

"An accused person has the right to know the names of the accusers," said Morgan. "Don't you agree?"

"Of course," said Mr Marsh. "It's a fundamental part of our system of justice."

"Well?" said Morgan.

"Mr Parsons, Mrs Meyer, and Mr Higgenbottom," said Mr Marsh, barely choking the names out.

"I can see why you were concerned," said Morgan. "They're three of Langford's leading citizens."

"I hope you don't think that influenced me," said Mr Marsh. "I like to think that in this school, all parents are equally respected."

"I like to think so too," said Morgan.

"Well, it's been a pleasure, as always, chatting with you, Ms Swift," said Mr Marsh. "I hope you don't mind my cutting into your lunch-time."

"Not at all," said Morgan, rising to leave. "I'd like to thank you, in fact. I always like to know what's going on. And this conversation has been most enlightening."

That day another person, too, was out to offer Morgan enlightenment.

Morgan had barely arrived home after school when her phone rang.

She recognized the accented voice at once.

Yang.

"Miss Swift, or as I imagine you prefer to be called, Ms Swift, I have good news for you. I have an opening in one of my classes. Since you seem so interested in my centre, I thought you might like to attend. I am always happy to have a truly seroius student, even though it means bending my usual rules."

"Why, thank you very much," said Morgan.

"I will see you in an hour, then," said Yang.

"See you," promised Morgan.

After she hung up, Morgan prepared herself to see Yang.

This would be the experiment she needed to

get the proof she was looking for. The way to turn her suspicion of what Yang was doing into a certainty.

There was just one hitch.

In this experiment she would be the guinea pig.

Chapter 14

"Since you're my two partners in the investigation, I thought you'd like to see the result of my experiment with Yang – or rather, listen to it," Morgan told Jenny and Sally.

Morgan had asked the two girls to come to her place that Monday night. The girls' parents were told that the visit was to get help in a chemistry project. But instead of looking at test tubes, Jenny and Sally were staring at Morgan's tape machine and wondering what was about to come out of it.

"Good thing I picked up this miniature recorder last time I was in Japan," said Morgan. "It would have been a nuisance to have to run out and buy one, and I really needed it when I went to Yang's."

"To get the evidence on tape – so people would believe you," said Jenny, nodding.

"Not only that," said Morgan. "There was also a good chance I'd need to listen to it myself – to find out what happened. I couldn't trust my memory after Sally showed me what Yang could do to a person's memory."

Sally opened her mouth to protest – but stayed silent as Morgan's finger came to rest on the playback button.

"I started the tape as I went into the private room with Yang," Morgan said, and then pressed the button to let the tape do the rest of the talking.

The machine was excellent, the tape high quality. Morgan and Yang sounded as if they were facing each other that very moment in Morgan's apartment.

"*I must stress that I need your total cooperation, Morgan,*" Yang said. "*I can call you Morgan, can't I? We are now teacher and student. You must accept that status.*"

"*Of course I do,*" said Morgan in a humble voice.

"*Good,*" said Yang. "*Now do exactly what I say.*"

"*I will,*" said Morgan.

"*With no mental reservations,*" said Yang.

"*With no mental reservations,*" echoed Morgan.

"*Very Good,*" said Yang. "*You have the idea. Now follow my instructions. Look into the pure light of the candle flame.*"

"*I am,*" said Morgan.

"*Let your mind fill with that light,*" said Yang, his voice gaining in power. "*Now there is only that light in your mind, and the sound of my voice. Light. And my voice. Light. And my voice. Telling you what to do. Telling you what you must do. Telling you what you are doing. What you are doing is letting go of your mind. Your mind is vanishing. All there is are my words. My words, telling you what to do . . .*"

Suddenly Yang's voice was cut off as Morgan pressed the stop button and said sharply, "Sally! Snap out of it!"

"Wha –?" Sally said, and then grinned sheepishly. "I guess I was going under, huh?

Just hearing the sound of Yang's voice."

"During the first hypnosis session he had with you," said Morgan, "he probably programmed you to respond to his voice alone. Maybe it might be safer from here on to tell you myself what happened. You can probably guess, anyway. Yang told me I would have no further interest in his activities and I would forget everything I've learned about him so far. I have to admit, he's really a master hypnotist. It was all I could do to battle his technique."

"I still don't understand one thing," said Jenny.

"What's that?" said Morgan.

"Why does Yang want to hypnotize kids?" Jenny asked. "What does he stand to gain?"

"We have to do a bit of deduction to figure that out," said Morgan. "The first thing to remember is that the power of a hypnotist is limited. He can't force you to do something you really don't want to do. So we can assume that the kids under his control had some kind of yearning to do what he asked them to do."

"And what was it?" asked Sally, leaning forward. "I'm one of those kids. What was I commanded to do?"

"Let's remember what you did do," said Morgan. "First you questioned me about my past. Then you went through my flat to find out any secrets about me that you could. You were naturally curious about me, and Yang used the curiosity as his tool to hunt for anything he could use as a weapon against me."

"And the other kids?" asked Jenny. "What did Yang have them looking for?"

88

"What do Amy and Carl and Sam have in common?" said Morgan. "Think."

"They're all in your class?" said Sally tentatively.

"That was just a coincidence," said Morgan. "A lucky coincidence. Otherwise, I'd never have spotted anything wrong with them. But what else do they have in common?"

Sally looked at Jenny. Jenny looked at Sally. They both shrugged and shook their heads.

"I guess we're just dumb," said Jenny.

"No, you're just not adults – and it's something that's important to adults rather than kids," said Morgan. "Amy and Carl and Sam all have parents who have important positions in the community, and sizable bank accounts. Put that together, add the fact that kids are naturally curious about their parents' pasts, and what do you think Yang could use those kids for?"

Jenny and Sally came up with the answer at the same time.

"Blackmail!"

"Very good," said Morgan. "Now we just have to find our –"

The ringing of the phone interrupted her.

It was Patrick O'Connor.

"Hope I didn't disturb you, but I just figured out who this Yang guy is, and I thought you'd want to know."

"You are so right," said Morgan.

"I checked into the private mental hospital you were locked up in," said O'Connor. "When I tried to find out who owned it, all I came up with was the name of a dummy corporation. But then I learned who the previous owner of record was, and the name rang a bell. I suddenly knew where I had seen Yang's face before."

"Where?" asked Morgan.

"In the newspapers, about four years ago. He was called John Dietrich then. Dr John Dietrich. A very successful psychotherapist – until his use of hypnosis got him involved in a lawsuit. He lost the lawsuit, his professional standing, his patients – and he disappeared. Until now. Look, I'd be careful in going after him if I were you. I talked to someone who used to know him, and apparently he's right on the edge of being wacko."

"Thanks, Pat," said Morgan. "If there's anything I can ever do for you, let me know."

"For starters, you can come back to New York for that date," said O'Connor. "Once you're here, I'm sure I'll be able to think of a few more things."

"I'll see if I can pencil it into my schedule," said Morgan, smiling.

After she hung up, she told Jenny and Sally what she had learned.

"Now all we have to do is expose him and drive him out of town," said Morgan. "We can even put him behind bars if we can get one of the parents he's been blackmailing to press charges against him."

"You think he's found things he can blackmail them with?" said Jenny.

"I'm sure he has," said Morgan. "He must have enough power over them to force them to do what he tells them. That's why all three of them complained about me to the school. When I heard about the complaints, I began to realize what he was doing."

"Now I see why he admitted me into his advanced class," said Sally, "It was just after he learned that I knew you well enough to get into your confidence." She paused, and a look of concern passed over her face. "But I'm still his tool, aren't I? I mean, he still has control of my mind, right?" She shuddered. "I'm scared."

"Don't be," Morgan said. "The effects of hypnosis wear off unless the hypnosis is re-enforced. His power over you and all the other kids is fading. That power will disappear – just like Yang will."

Just then a voice sounded in the room.

An unmistakable voice.

Instinctively everyone looked at the tape machine before they realized the voice was real.

"I am afraid you are wrong, Morgan. It is not I who will disappear. It is the three of you."

Yang walked into the room through the door he had swung open. His towering form seemed to dwarf everything in it, including the gun in his huge hand.

Chapter 15

"You should get a better lock for your door, Morgan," Yang said. "It is absurdly easy to get a master key for the model you have."

He dropped the key on the table while keeping his gun on Morgan and Jenny and Sally.

"All three of you, line up against the wall, with your hands on your heads," he said.

"I don't know what you think you're doing, busting in here like this," Morgan said as they followed his orders. "We were just going over a chemistry project when you –"

"Spare me your pitiful pretending," Yang said. "You are not the only one who can use the marvels of our electronic age. You might have your tape recorder, but I have something far better – thanks to Sally here. You are a most capable assistant, Sally – much more reliable than those clods who let Morgan and Jenny escape in New York."

"Me? What did I do?" Sally asked, sounding as if she dreaded to hear the answer.

"You followed your instructions," Yang said, and went to where the portrait of Morgan's Renaissance prince hung. He swung the picture out from the wall to display a small device fastened to the back of the frame. "Before you started your search of this apartment, you did a perfect job of bugging it." Yang took a miniature listening device from his pocket. "I have heard every word all of you said here this evening."

"Oh, *no*," said Sally.

"Oh, *yes*, "said Yang. "You see, Morgan, you should not have underestimated the power I have over my students – just as you should not have meddled in my work. But I suppose such interference is the cross I must bear for refusing to follow the rules made for small minds by small minds. I was driven from my profession for daring to free patients from their crippling doubts and fears through my advanced techniques of hypnosis. The fools who called themselves my colleagues refused to recognize my achievement – just as you, Morgan, would not accept the remarkable progress my students made."

"It's the price of the progress that I don't accept," said Morgan. "Those kids might have got rid of their hangups, but they didn't do it through their own efforts. They did it by becoming slaves to you."

"Some people are born to be masters, and others to serve," said Yang. "To put it a way you might better understand, Morgan, some of us are born to be teachers, and others students. Indeed, it's a pity you and I find ourselves on opposing sides. We really are two of the same kind."

"Never," said Morgan. "As far as I'm concerned, there are no teachers, no students, just people who have different things to teach each other and learn from each other."

"If you insist," said Yang, shrugging. "But right now *I* am the teacher, and the lesson you are about to learn will be unpleasant."

"What do you plan to do, shoot us?" said Morgan, refusing to look scared. "You might be crazy, but you can't be that crazy. You'd never get away with it."

"Crazy am I?" said Yang, and for the first time emotion shattered his calm mask. Rage flashed from his eyes. "You will see how crazy I am, just as the world will. My genius will soon be recognized – by those who now condemn me. With a little more time, a little more money, I will produce irrefutable proof of the success of my work – and I will have that time and money when you are out of the way."

"Then your blackmailing paid off?" said Morgan, stalling for time.

"Of course, as I knew it would," said Yang with satisfaction. "I knew the parents would have secrets they were afraid of. People who reach high-enough positions are always vulnerable to small things that can bring them tumbling down. I learned *that* when one miserable complaint from one pitifully insignificant patient wrecked my career. For Mr Parsons, there was a shoplifting charge when he was a teenager. A small thing – but it could threaten his post at the bank. For Mrs Meyer, it was a reprimand for drug use in college – just the kind of youthful folly that could poison her medical reputation. And for Mr Higgenbottom, it was being jailed in a violent student demonstration in the sixties. How that must haunt him these days as he preaches nonviolence in his political campaigns."

"Such small things to be afraid of," Morgan said.

"Young people aren't the only ones who are crippled by their fears," said Yang, smiling. Then his smile widened. "But you, Morgan, and you, Jenny, don't have to feel silly being afraid. You have something very real to fear."

Then he said in a different tone, a deep bass voice, "*Sally! Attention!*"

As Morgan and Jenny watched in horror, Sally dropped her hands to her sides and stood stiffly at attention. She looked like a mechanical soldier, and her voice was mechanical as well. "Yes, I am listening."

"*Sally*," said Morgan sharply.

"*Wake up*," said Jenny, desperation in her voice as she saw what was happening to her friend.

"Don't waste your breath," Yang said. "You cannot disturb her trance now that I am present. She is in my power completely. She can hear only me."

He turned to Sally. "Where does Morgan keep her chemistry equipment?"

"In her shoulder bag, on the table there," Sally said in the same dead voice.

"Take it out and set it up on the table," Yang said.

As Sally followed his orders Yang said to Morgan, "You really should be more careful in doing chemistry experiments with your students. It will be quite careless, not to say irresponsible, when you and Jenny are overcome by deadly gas you accidentally let escape – leaving only Sally to tell the story to the police. Sally will be inconsolable because it was she who did the actual mixing of the chemicals, as

95

her fingerprints on the test tubes will prove. She will be able to tell the police only that, and nothing more." He then said to Sally, "Did you hear? And will you obey?"

"I heard – and I will obey," said Sally, taking the chemistry kit out of Morgan's shoulder bag.

"You'll never get away with this," said Morgan.

"Yes, I will," said Yang, watching as Sally set up the contents of the kit on the table. "I only regret, Morgan, that you will not be able to see it."

With his gun still trained on Morgan and Jenny, he went to the table and inspected Sally's work. "Very good, Sally. I see that Morgan has all the chemicals we need for our little experiment. I am sure it will be quite successful. During my medical studies, chemistry was one of my strongest subjects. I remember it quite well."

As he bent over the set, Morgan began to edge away from the wall. There might be just a slim chance to get close enough to make a quick charge, deliver a sneak karate punch.

Instantly Yang's gun snapped into firing position. "Don't even think of doing anything foolish, Morgan. I will not hesitate to fire. I have nothing to lose. And if you force me to use my gun, Sally will die along with the rest of you. I don't think either you or Jenny want to be responsible for her death."

Morgan backed up again against the wall. She knew Yang was not lying about what he would do. He was that close to madness. He also was not lying about his knowledge of chemistry. He did not hesitate as he told Sally what chemicals to prepare to mix when he gave the word.

"Sally and I will wait by the open door while the gas spreads throughout the room," said Yang, after making sure Sally had everything in order. "We will watch it take effect when it reaches you. I promise, death will come quickly and painlessly. And if you make a move to escape, remember that not only you two but also Sally will die."

He turned to Sally. "Do you hear and obey?"

"I hear – and will obey," Sally said.

Desperately Morgan tried to think of a way out as Jenny looked to her for salvation.

"I'm sorry, Jenny," was all she could say.

"What a fool you were to pit your mind against mine," said Yang triumphantly.

Then he turned to Sally, waiting beside him for his command, and said, "*Now!*"

═══════ Chapter 16 ═══════

"*Now!*"

The note of triumph in Yang's voice swelled like a note played on a violin.

Then, suddenly, it turned to a hideous screech of agony.

"*Owwwww!*"

Yang's gun dropped to the floor. Both his hands went to his face to cover his eyes – but they were too late to stop the damage that had been done.

His blinded eyes could not see what had happened – but Morgan and Jenny could.

Sally had flung the contents of a test tube directly in Yang's face.

A minute later, after Morgan had the gun in her hand, covering Yang, Sally explained. "I'm glad I was paying attention in class when you taught us about the effects of that acid. Do you think it'll blind him permanently?"

"No," said Morgan. "It should wear off in a short while. Good work, Sally. You had Yang totally fooled. And me, too."

"I didn't think I'd fool *you*," said Sally. "I mean, you did tell me that a hypnotist couldn't force me to do anything I really didn't want to do. As soon as Yang told me to kill you and Jenny, I snapped out of his control."

"I should have known," agreed Morgan. "But sometimes it's hard to remember what you know to be true when the opposite seems to be happening before your very eyes."

"I'm just surprised a guy who knows as much about hypnotism as Yang tried to make me do it," said Sally.

"Yang overestimated his power," said Morgan. "A common mistake with petty tyrants. They may succeed to a point, but then they go too far. He learned what they all learn – that when you push people too far they rebel."

"It was just an accident," said Yang, blinking his eyes as his vision began to clear. "I must have been careless in my technique."

"You'll have a lot of time to figure out where you made a mistake," said Morgan. "At least ten years in prison for attempted murder, among other things."

"Don't be foolish," said Yang. "If you call the police, I'll reveal what I know about the kids' parents. I'll make a deal. Let me get out of town, and I'll keep quiet."

"You'll keep quiet, anyway," said Morgan. "Do you know what the penalty for blackmail is? Added on to other charges against you, it could put you in jail until well into the next century. I have a different deal for you. Don't mention the kids' parents, and I won't mention what you were doing to them."

"Let me think, I need time to think," said Yang.

"You have about ten minutes," said Morgan as she picked up the phone. "It should take about that long for the police to get here."

"Okay, you win, it's a deal," said Yang, his eyes glowering, his towering form rigid with anger. "But don't think you have seen the last of me. This is merely a temporary setback. I will find a way to get out and fulfill my destiny."

"I'm sure you'll try," said Morgan. "As a Franciscan monk once told me, one never completely defeats evil; one must constantly battle against it." She started to dial the police. "Let's just say I won this round."

Ten minutes later two uniformed policemen arrived.

"I'm afraid you'll have to come down to the station, Miss Swift, to press charges," said one of them as the other snapped handcuffs on Yang.

"What about us?" asked Jenny.

"You two had better get back home pronto – if you want to be rested for the snap test I'm springing in class tomorrow," said Morgan.

Sally and Jenny stood on the sidewalk as Morgan climbed into her Mercedes 190 to follow the squad car to the station. The convertible top was open, and the last sight the girls had of Morgan was the glint of the silver streak in her hair as her car moved under a streetlight. Then Sally and Jenny started walking home through the cool night under a star-filled spring sky.

It took a few minutes for Sally to break the awkward silence between them.

"Hey, you know, I'm sorry I acted kind of creepy to you about Yang's classes and all," she said. "I mean, it was really dumb of me. Like, you're the best friend I have, and I totally forgot it."

"That's okay," said Jenny. "You were under

100

Yang's influence. I understand. And I feel a little guilty too, for thinking you were acting that way on your own. I should have known better. I should have known *you* better. You're my best friend too."

"Still your best friend?" said Sally.

"Still my best friend," said Jenny.

"Thanks, pal," said Sally, and at the same moment they both broke into grins, embarrassed and happy at the same time.

They walked half a block more, the silence between them warm and comfortable now.

Then Sally said, "You know, there's one thing I still regret about this case."

"What's that?" asked Jenny.

"That you and Morgan busted in on me so soon when I was going through Morgan's apartment," said Sally. "A little while longer, and I might have found out who her secret boyfriend was. Or where she was born and raised. Or whether she has brothers and sisters. Or even why she's teaching at Coolidge High. Yang was right about me. There is a lot about her that I'd do almost anything to know."

"She is mysterious, isn't she?" agreed Jenny. "A mystery who solves mysteries."

"She's a mystery *we* definitely have to solve," Sally said. "Maybe we can do it on our next adventure with her."

"*If* there's another adventure with her," said Jenny. She paused, then grinned and said, "But I guess if we stick around her, we don't have to worry about *that*."

HIPPO CLASSICS

If you have enjoyed this book, why not move on to some of the following books from the Hippo Classics list. Each one a great read – and such good value!

LITTLE WOMEN	Louisa M Alcott	£1.00
THE HOUND OF THE BASKERVILLES	Sir Arthur Conan Doyle	£1.00
THE WIND IN THE WILLOWS	Kenneth Grahame	£1.00
THE RAILWAY CHILDREN	E Nesbit	£1.00
HEIDI	Johanna Spyri	£1.00
TREASURE ISLAND	Robert L Stevenson	£1.00
THE ADVENTURES OF TOM SAWYER	Mark Twain	£1.00
AROUND THE WORLD IN EIGHTY DAYS	Jules Verne	£1.00

You'll find these and many more fun Hippo books at your local bookseller, or you can order them direct. Just send off to *Customer Services, Hippo Books, Westfield Road, Southam, Leamington Spa, Warwickshire CV33 0JH*, not forgetting to enclose a cheque or postal order for the price of the book(s) plus 30p for postage and packing.

HIPPO BOOKS FOR OLDER READERS

If you enjoy a good read, look out for all the Hippo books that are available for older readers. You'll find gripping adventure stories, romance novels, spooky ghost stories and all sorts of fun fiction.

CHEERLEADERS NO 2: GETTING EVEN	Christopher Pike	£1.25
CHEERLEADERS NO 3: RUMOURS	Cároline B Cooney	£1.25
ANIMAL INN 1: PETS ARE FOR KEEPS	Virginia Vail	£1.50
MEGASTAR	Jean Ure	£1.50
SOMERSAULTS	Michael Hardcastle	£1.50
THE LITTLE GYMNAST	Sheila Haigh	£1.25
CREEPS	Tim Schoch	£1.50
THE GREAT FLOOD MYSTERY	Jane Curry	£1.75
GET LAVINIA GOODBODY!	Roger Collinson	£1.25
AM I GOING WITH YOU?	Thurley Fowler	£1.25
THE KARATE KID: PART II	B B Hiller	£1.25
KEVIN AND THE IRON POODLE	J K Hooper	£1.25

You'll find these and many more fun Hippo books at your local bookseller, or you can order them direct. Just send off to *Customer Services, Hippo Books, Westfield Road, Southam, Leamington Spa, Warwickshire CV33 OJH*, not forgetting to enclose a cheque or postal order for the price of the book(s) plus 30p per book for postage and packing.

HIPPO CHEERLEADERS

Have you met the girls and boys from Tarenton High?
Follow the lives and loves of the six who form the school
Cheerleading team.

CHEERLEADERS NO 2:
GETTING EVEN   Christopher Pike   £1.25
CHEERLEADERS NO 3:
RUMOURS   Caroline B Cooney   £1.25
CHEERLEADERS NO 4:
FEUDING   Lisa Norby   £1.25
CHEERLEADERS NO 5:
ALL THE WAY   Caroline B Cooney   £1.25
CHEERLEADERS NO 6:
SPLITTING   Jennifer Sarasin   £1.25
CHEERLEADERS NO 7:
FLIRTING   Diane Hoh   £1.25
CHEERLEADERS NO 8:
FORGETTING   Lisa Norby   £1.25
CHEERLEADERS NO 9:
PLAYING GAMES   Jody Sorenson   £1.25
CHEERLEADERS NO 11:
CHEATING   Jennifer Sarasin   £1.25
CHEERLEADERS NO 12:
STAYING TOGETHER   Diane Hoh   £1.25
CHEERLEADERS NO 13:
HURTING   Lisa Norby   £1.25
CHEERLEADERS NO 14:
LIVING IT UP   Jennifer Sarasin   £1.25
CHEERLEADERS NO 15:
WAITING   Jody Sorenson   £1.25

CHEERLEADERS NO 16:		
IN LOVE	Carol Stanley	£1.50
CHEERLEADERS NO 17:		
TAKING RISKS	Anne Reynolds	£1.50
CHEERLEADERS NO 18:		
LOOKING GOOD	Carol Ellis	£1.50
CHEERLEADERS NO 19:		
MAKING IT	Susan Blake	£1.50
CHEERLEADERS NO 20:		
STARTING OVER	Patricia Aks & Lisa Norby	£1.50
CHEERLEADERS NO 21:		
PULLING TOGETHER	Diane Hoh	£1.50
CHEERLEADERS NO 22:		
RIVALS	Ann E Steinke	£1.50
CHEERLEADERS NO 23:		
PROVING IT	Diane Hoh	£1.50
CHEERLEADERS NO 24:		
GOING STRONG	Carol Ellis	£1.50
CHEERLEADERS NO 25:		
STEALING SECRETS	Anne E Steinke	£1.50

You'll find these and many more fun Hippo books at your local bookseller, or you can order them direct. Just send off to *Customer Services, Hippo Books, Westfield Road, Southam, Leamington Spa, Warwickshire CV33 0JH*, not forgetting to enclose a cheque of postal order for the price of the book(s) plus 30p for postage and packing.

HIPPO BESTSELLERS

If you enjoyed this book, why not look out for other bestselling Hippo titles. You'll find gripping novels, fun activity books, fascinating non-fiction, crazy humour and sensational poetry books for all ages and tastes.

THE GHOSTBUSTERS STORYBOOK	Anne Digby	£2.50
SNOOKERED	Michael Hardcastle	£1.50
BENJI THE HUNTED	Walt Disney Company	£2.25
NELLIE AND THE DRAGON	Elizabeth Lindsay	£1.75
ALIENS IN THE FAMILY	Margaret Mahy	£1.50
HARRIET AND THE CROCODILES	Martin Waddell	£1.25
MAKE ME A STAR 1: PRIME TIME	Susan Beth Pfeffer	£1.50
THE SPRING BOX	Troy Alexander	£2.25
SLEUTH!	Sherlock Ransford	£1.50
THE SPOOKTACULAR JOKE BOOK	Theodore Freek	£1.25
ROLAND RAT'S RODENT JOKE BOOK		£1.25
THE LITTLE VAMPIRE	Angela Sommer-Bodenberg	£1.25
POSTMAN PAT AND THE GREENDALE GHOST	John Cunliffe	£1.50
POSTMAN PAT AND THE CHRISTMAS PUDDING	John Cunliffe	£1.50

You'll find these and many more fun Hippo books at your local bookseller, or you can order them direct. Just send off to *Customer Services, Hippo Books, Westfield Road, Southam, Leamington Spa, Warwickshire CV33 0JH*, not forgetting to enclose a cheque or postal order for the price of the book(s) plus 30p per book for postage and packing.

HIPPO ACTIVITY BOOKS

Feeling bored? Get into some of these activity books on the Hippo list – from Postman Pat to Defenders of the Earth, there is plenty of fun to be had by all!

THE DISNEY QUIZ AND PUZZLE BOOK	The Walt Disney Company	£0.99
THE DISNEY QUIZ AND PUZZLE BOOK II	The Walt Disney Company	£1.25
MILES OF FUN	Penny Kitchenham	£1.95
ADVENTURE IN SPACE	Janet McKellar and Jenny Bullough	£1.95
THE HAUNTED CASTLE		£1.95
COUNTRYSIDE ACTIVITY BOOK		£1.95
THE DINOSAUR FUN BOOK	Gillian Osband	£1.95
THE ANTI-COLOURING BOOK	Susan Striker	£2.75
THE MAGIC MIRROR BOOK	Marion Walter	£1.75
THE SECOND MAGIC MIRROR BOOK	Marion Walter	£1.50
THE INTERPLANETARY TOY BOOK	J Alan Williams	£2.25
THE SUMMER ACTIVITY BOOK	Hannah Glease	£2.25
THE HOLIDAY FUN BOOK		£1.95
POSTMAN PAT'S SONGBOOK	Bryan Daly	£1.75
THE SPRING BOOK	Troy Alexander	£2.25
THE DEEP FREEZE ADVENTURE COLOURING BOOK		£0.75

You'll find these and many more fun Hippo books at your local bookseller, or you can order them direct. Just send off to *Customer Services, Hippo Books, Westfield Road, Southam, Leamington Spa, Warwickshire CV33 0JH*, not forgetting to enclose a cheque or postal order for the price of the book(s) plus 30p per book for postage and packing.

MORGAN SWIFT

Morgan Swift's twenty-four, stunningly beautiful,
independent, a great runner, and a fabulous science
teacher. And she has the knack of finding trouble – and
getting out of it!

MORGAN SWIFT AND THE MINDMASTER

Morgan Swift has an extraordinary ability – she has the
power of second sight. And when her mental powers
warn her that some of her pupils at Coolidge High are in
trouble, she decides to investigate. It's not long before
she finds the culprit – a cult leader called Yang who's
been giving the kids extra coaching after school . . .

MORGAN SWIFT AND THE TRAIL OF THE JAGUAR

Morgan Swift's two pupils, Jenny Wu and Sally
Jackson, are thrilled to be going on holiday with their
favourite teacher. And they can't believe their luck when
an old friend of Morgan's, the attractive Tom Saunders,
invites them to go on an ultra-secret archaeological dig
in the South American jungle. But when things start to
go wrong, they turn to their teacher to find out exactly
what's going on in the jungle . . .

Watch out for more titles in the thrilling
MORGAN SWIFT series:

MORGAN SWIFT AND THE LAKE OF DIAMONDS
MORGAN SWIFT AND THE RIDDLE OF THE SPHINX